MARRY IN HASTE

He married her ... but did he trust her...?

Whilst accompanying her aunt to a ball in Bath, Amelia Ravenscroft overhears a young man declare that he is looking for a bride. As she is desperate to escape the attentions of her lecherous cousin Sir Bernard, she impulsively offers her hand in marriage and discovers that the young man is James, Viscount Demarr. They elope to Gretna Green, and then return to his country estate, but James begins to have doubts about Amelia's past. It is not until Amelia is once again threatened by Sir Bernard that James acknowledges his true feelings.

D1614513

MARRY IN HASTE

Marry In Haste

by

Christina Courtenay

Dales Large Print Books
Long Preston, North Yorkshire,
BD23 4ND, England.

British Library Cataloguing in Publication Data.

Courtenay, Christina
    Marry in haste.

    A catalogue record of this book is
    available from the British Library

    ISBN   978-1-84262-706-8 pbk

First published in Great Britain in 2008 by
D. C. Thomson & Co. Ltd.

Published in Large Print 2009 by arrangement with
Pia Tapper Fenton

Dales Large Print is an imprint of Library Magna Books Ltd.

Printed and bound in Great Britain by
T.J. (International) Ltd., Cornwall, PL28 8RW

CHAPTER ONE

Amelia Ravenscroft sat shivering on a small bench in the furthest corner of the cold terrace while everyone else enjoyed themselves inside the ballroom. She knew that she couldn't stay there forever, but nothing would make her go back inside a moment before she had to. She would rather freeze to death.

The members of the *ton* currently residing in Bath had gathered for their usual round of matchmaking and flirting, which was all determined by wealth and social status. Amelia no longer had either, being a poor relation dependent on her aunt's goodwill, and consequently they treated her as if she didn't exist. It was infuriating and humiliating all at once and she was determined to have at least a short respite from playing the wallflower.

Lost in thought, she failed to notice that she was no longer alone on the terrace until a disembodied voice echoed across the expanse with some force, startling her.

'I need to marry, and I need to marry at once,' it declared.

Intrigued, Amelia peered through the darkness to see if she could discern the speaker. Two men were standing by the low parapet, lit from behind by the light spilling out of the French doors. She couldn't make out their features, but one was clearly agitated and began to pace back and forth.

'What am I to do? It's impossible, I tell you.'

'Well, surely James, it can't be that difficult to find a female to marry at short notice?' the calmer man said. 'After all, you're a personable fellow and heir to an earldom no less. There was a time when all the young ladies were throwing themselves at you, as I recall.'

'That was before the scandal.' The one called James continued his pacing. 'You know as well as I do that any female who married me would have to be besotted to the point of madness to put up with all the slights and snubs she would be sure to receive. No-one in polite society will so much as have me under their roof. I'm only here tonight because Mrs Cruikshank is my mother's cousin and she took pity on me.'

'Hmm, tricky situation. Why the hurry?'

'My grandfather is dying. He told me the doctors give him only a few months, maybe a year at best and he wants to see me settled and with an heir if possible before he goes. The old curmudgeon was the only one to stand by me at the time of the scandal, how can I refuse his dying wish?'

'Why not elope with someone? That's the fastest way, surely.'

Amelia stifled a gasp. Elopement was a serious step for anyone to take, the two people involved would have to be truly desperate, but how she wished someone would try to elope with her. Anything would be better than spending another night under her aunt's roof.

'No, that requires wooing first, and I haven't the time.'

'What about the daughter of a city merchant then? They'll happily overlook anything to have a title in the family.'

'Not an option. My future wife has to be of a good family, grandfather insisted on that. I wondered … you wouldn't happen to know of any indigent lady who might jump at the chance to become Viscountess? A governess or lady's companion perhaps? I don't normally come across their kind in the sort of circles I move in, so I'm at my wit's end.'

'Sorry, but not offhand. Give me a few weeks and maybe my wife could help me find someone?'

A deep sigh reached Amelia's ears. She knew she shouldn't be listening to this conversation, should have declared her presence immediately in fact, but she found herself riveted and couldn't have moved if her life depended on it.

'Thank you, but that will probably be too

late. Never mind, it was a long shot. I appreciate you listening to my ravings, but now you had better go back into the ballroom and do the pretty to your beloved. I shall stay here for a while I think, save my aunt the embarrassment of having to introduce me to anyone else.'

Silence descended on the terrace, and although the sounds of a ball in full swing emanated from the open windows, to Amelia it felt as if they came from a different world, one to which she did not belong.

The man who had stayed outside leaned on the balustrade and lit a cheroot. She could see the tip of it glowing from time to time and the sharp aroma of tobacco wafted past her nose. His features were still hidden by the darkness, but something in his voice had made her feel for him in his predicament. He sounded almost as despairing as she herself felt this evening.

A thought struck her, so daring she almost cried out loud, then she shook her head. No, she could never be that bold. But then again, what did she have to lose?

Before she could think any further, she jumped to her feet and half-ran over to the man by the balustrade. Obviously startled by the unexpected footfall behind him, he turned swiftly, and she saw him frown. 'What...?' he began, then collected himself. 'I beg your pardon, ma'am, I did not hear you come out.' He bowed stifled and threw his cheroot into the flower bed below, then made as if to step around her to return inside.

Amelia stopped him by the simple expedient of taking a step in the same direction. 'I ... I didn't come out exactly,' she stammered nervously. 'I was sitting on the bench over there,' she pointed towards the shadows behind them, 'and I'm afraid I overheard your conversation with your friend.'

His eyes narrowed a fraction and he looked at her more closely. 'I see. And did you learn anything of value?' he asked sarcastically.

'Well, yes, I mean no ... I mean, oh I don't know how to say this, but...' She took a deep breath and the words came tumbling out in a rush. 'I will marry you if you wish.'

The man stared at her as if she had suddenly grown two heads and Amelia cringed. She couldn't understand what had possessed her to do this, she must be out of her mind, but having gone this far, she decided she may as well continue.

'I don't care for society at all, so I wouldn't mind being snubbed, and I come from a very good family. My grandfather was the Marquess of Ravenscroft.'

'Was he indeed? If that is so, then why are you out here on your own proposing marriage to a stranger? I take it you don't know who I am?'

'Erm, no. No I don't, but the thing is, it doesn't matter. Anyone will do.'

'How flattering. That makes me feel a lot better,' he drawled.

Amelia took another deep breath. This was not going at all well and had it not been so dark, the man would have seen that she was blushing from head to toe. 'What I meant was, I need to marry too and I cannot afford to be choosy. As long as you can give me a roof over my head and a ring on my finger, that is all that matters.'

He regarded her in silence, then shook his head as if he couldn't believe this was happening. 'Tell me, what is it you need to escape from? I take it there is a good reason for your desperation? Are you with child?'

'No!' Amelia was horrified. 'Of course not. That's the whole point – I'm trying to avoid being seduced out of wedlock.'

'Perhaps you should start at the beginning? I'm finding myself increasingly muddled by your explanations. Come, let us sit on your hidden bench.' He grabbed her elbow and steered her none too gently to the dark corner and sat down. 'Now then, first things first – I'm James Jolyon Winholt, Viscount Demarr, and you are?'

'Amelia Ravenscroft.'

'Very well, now tell me all.'

Amelia took a deep breath and launched into her story. 'My father, Colonel Ravenscroft, died a year ago. He … he shot himself, having incurred too many gambling debts. I was left penniless, but my aunt by marriage, that is my mother's sister-in-law, Lady Marsh, took me in as she needed a companion for her daughter, Maria. It turned out that she also needed a housekeeper, so I took on those duties as well and a few others besides.

'All was well until her son, Sir Bernard, came home to rusticate as he put it. For some reason he decided I was fair game and began to pursue me, making my life very difficult. I have avoided him so far, but he grows more daring with each day and soon I fear I will not be able to keep him at bay.'

Lord Demarr frowned. 'But surely your aunt can put a stop to this? It would not be in her interest to have her son seduce you.'

Amelia shook her head. 'No, she knows what he is doing and is turning a blind eye. He is her favourite, you see, she always wants him to have whatever he desires. I think, if the worst came to the worst, she would simply send me away, and then what would I do?'

'It sounds very callous to me. You are sure your cousin doesn't mean to marry you?'

'No, indeed. Why should he if he can have what he wants anyway? He's forever broke, so he needs to marry an heiress. Besides, I wouldn't marry him if he was the last man on earth, he makes my skin crawl.'

'And how do you know I won't have the same effect on you?'

Amelia blinked. 'Well, I … I hadn't thought of that.'

'Perhaps we should put it to the test?' Without further ado, his lordship pulled Amelia into his embrace and gave her a soft kiss, full on the lips. She froze, expecting to be frightened, but the strange thing was that she felt none of the revulsion Bernard's attempts at kissing her had provoked, quite the opposite, and when Lord Demarr stopped, her lips were left tingling. It was the strangest feeling.

His lordship suddenly pulled her to her feet and dragged her over to where light was spilling out from one of the tall windows.

He studied her face and then nodded, as if satisfied with what he saw. 'Very well, Miss Ravenscroft, I think you passed the test. I shall need to confirm your story somehow, but if you are telling me the truth, I see no reason why we shouldn't marry. After all, the matter is urgent.'

Amelia stilled, unable to utter so much as a word. In the light she saw his features clearly for the first time, and realised what an attractive man he was. Tall, with a shock of dark hair that was too long to be fashionable, his face looked like it had been sculpted by Michelangelo or his like. She could not see the colour of his eyes, but his gaze pierced her to the core. Powerful shoulders and legs added to the look of determination and she almost quaked in her shoes. What had she got herself into?

'I...' she began, but her tongue refused to form the words.

'Can you meet me out here in another hour or so?' he asked, bringing her back to her senses.

'Yes, I suppose so.'

'Good. I will go and make some enquiries, then meet you here. Until then...' He took one of her hands in his and bent to brush it with his lips, 'Adieu.'

As James walked away from the strange, but compelling female on the terrace, he wondered if he was insane to even think of accepting her proposal. She was clearly desperate, and although her story rang true, he could not but wonder at her motives. Surely, if she did not want to remain under her aunt's roof, she could apply for a post as a governess or companion? But he knew that without references, she may not be very successful.

She was not exactly the sort of female he had envisaged as his wife. Although her face had been pretty enough, she had worn her silver-blonde hair in unbecoming ringlets that looked none too clean. She was small and plump, rather too plump round the middle for his liking, and the dress she had been wearing had done nothing to enhance her attractions – quite the opposite in fact.

The material had resembled nothing so much as sackcloth and James was sure she couldn't have chosen a worse colour if she had tried. The nondescript sandy hue had made her already pale complexion seem ashen.

The point was, however, that he did not have the time to be fussy. As long as she fulfilled the criteria his grandfather had dictated, that was all that mattered. After all, it wasn't as though James intended to spend a great deal of time in her company. Once she was with child, he could leave her in the country while he went back to his usual pursuits.

He decided that, all things considered, perhaps Miss Ravenscroft would do very nicely indeed.

CHAPTER TWO

Amelia hurried back inside, suddenly anxious lest her aunt had missed her. She was required to see to her cousin, Maria's, every need, but fortunately the young lady was dancing when Amelia returned, and Lady Marsh was enjoying a cosy tête-a-tête with a particular crony of hers, discussing all the latest on-dits. No-one had noted Amelia's absence.

The next hour passed excruciatingly slowly, despite the lavish supper that was served after the supper dance. Since Amelia had not been partnered for this dance, there was no-one to lead her in and she was forced to eat with her aunt and that lady's friends. This didn't bother her much, for she was far too nervous to eat.

What on earth had got into her, she wondered. How could she have been so brazen as to propose marriage to a complete stranger? She knew nothing about him, he could be a cruel and vicious man and she could be letting herself in for a horrifying future. What was the scandal he had spoken of? Had he perhaps killed someone?

She brought her thoughts firmly under control and tried to think rationally. Surely he wouldn't be a free man if he was a murderer. It was more likely that the scandal had to do with either a woman, a duel or gambling, and none of those things troubled her unduly, except perhaps the last one. She would have to make sure he wasn't a gambler like her late father, or she would be left destitute once more.

Time dragged on and Amelia began to doubt that Lord Demarr would really meet her on the terrace again. Had it just been a ruse to rid himself of what he probably considered a demented female? She didn't know whether he had truly believed her or had only pretended.

At last the time came, and she excused herself to her aunt. Once out on the terrace, she stood for a moment to allow her eyes to adjust to the darkness. Then she saw a slight movement over by the bench. The Viscount was there before her.

'I'm sorry, I couldn't get away any earlier,' she apologised, slightly breathless with nerves.

'That is quite all right, I have only just arrived myself.'

He was silent for the longest time, and Amelia was beginning to think that he was trying to find a way of letting her down gently when he finally spoke. 'Well, I can't find any faults with your story,' he said. 'It seems everyone knows that your aunt is using you in return for your daily bread, even mistreating you according to some. Our hostess, Mrs Cruikshank, was especially forthcoming on the subject.'

'She and my aunt are not the best of friends. Truly, my situation is not as bad as all that, it was only when Bernard…'

'Ah, yes, your cousin. I have to tell you that he corroborated your story himself.'

'What? You asked him?' Amelia was aghast at the thought.

'No, no, I'm not such a sapskull as all that. I asked my friend, David, who apparently knows your cousin slightly, to joke with him about the blonde beauty he has living under his mother's roof, and believe it or not, the man actually had the nerve to hint that you were his mistress. He implied that you had thrown yourself at him ever since you arrived in the hope that he would marry you.'

Amelia nearly choked with rage. 'How dare he?' She stood up to go and confront the lying toad on the spot.

'Never mind,' his lordship put a soothing hand on her arm. 'He has unwittingly aided you in escaping his clutches. Let us put our heads together to frustrate him in his schemes.'

Before Amelia could react to this state-ment, Lord Demarr suddenly went down on one knee in front of her. 'Will you do me the honour of becoming my wife, Miss Ravens-croft?'

'Yes, yes of course.' Amelia felt herself blush again, although why she had no idea. After all, she was the one who had started all this, no time to turn coy now.

'Good,' said the Viscount matter-of-factly, sitting down beside her once more. 'Then all we have to decide is where and when to be married. Have you any suggestions.'

Amelia thought for a moment. 'I know this may sound very melodramatic,' she said hesitantly, 'but could we perhaps go to Gretna Green? I am only nineteen and my cousin is my legal guardian I believe. I shouldn't think he would willingly give his consent to this match.'

'Good point. Very well, then, Gretna Green it is. We can always pretend we fell in love at first sight, then no-one will question our going to Scotland to be married. The sooner, the better, as far as I am concerned. I shall make all the arrangements and let you know when all is ready. How can I contact you without anyone being the wiser?'

'Leave a message with Bootle, the butler. He has been very kind to me and is completely trustworthy. Please do not put anything in writing though.'

'Agreed.' He stood up, as if all was sorted to his satisfaction. 'Oh, I almost forgot. Do you like children?'

Amelia found herself blushing for a third time and turned her head away. 'Yes, I like them very much. If you are afraid I will not do my duty and produce an heir, I can assure you...'

'No, I wasn't worried about that, but I forgot to tell you that I already have two daughters, so you will be a step-mother. Can you cope with that?'

'Yes, I don't think that will be a problem. How old are they?'

'Six and four. They spend most of their time with the nanny, so they shouldn't trouble you unduly.'

'I see. Well, I look forward to meeting them. Erm, can I ask you a question?'

'Of course.'

'Do you gamble much?'

He smiled reassuringly. 'Never more than my finances can take, so please don't worry on that account. As my wife, you will never want for anything ever again.'

Amelia suppressed a sigh of relief. 'Thank you.' Whatever other faults he had, she felt sure she could cope with them.

'One other thing – please try not to bring too much luggage.' Lord Demarr glanced at her gown and shuddered. 'If you don't mind, I will buy you an entire new wardrobe.'

Amelia almost laughed out loud. What woman would mind being bought new clothes?

All she said was, 'As you wish.'

CHAPTER THREE

The following morning was one of the longest in Amelia's life, or so she thought. She tried to preserve her calm as she went about her daily duties, but she was in such a state of nervous anxiety that she was unusually pale and had to plead a headache when pressed as to the cause. Fortunately her aunt and cousin were both suffering from the effects of a very late night and were not inclined to question her further.

As for Bernard, he had spent the remainder of the night gambling and drinking and consequently spent most of the day in bed with a sore head.

'His temper's not improved by the fact that he lost heavily,' Bootle murmured to Amelia with a shake of his head. Instead of being able to go back to London with his winnings, Bernard now faced the prospect of having to kick his heels in his mother's house indefinitely.

When he finally emerged from his room towards late afternoon, however, the strange looks and smirks that came Amelia's way made her feel distinctly uneasy. As she could not guess what evil plan he was hatching, she could but wait and see.

Amelia sighed. After his last visit to Bath, she had come up with a plan which she hoped would put him off his pursuit of her. By adding layers of padding and numerous extra petticoats under her gown, she had transformed her normally trim figure into something that resembled a small barrel. She had adapted several of Lady Marsh's old gowns to fit, and as that lady favoured dull hues, this also helped to make Amelia's skin appear sallow. She had heard Bernard say that he abhorred fat females, but although he had made disparaging remarks about her altered shape upon his return, sadly it had not put him off completely.

She shook her head, there was no time to ponder this problem now, and with luck she would soon be married to Lord Demarr and thus safe from Bernard's lecherous advances. Amelia headed for the kitchen, to continue her work. There was always a lot to do, and she was therefore not best pleased when, a while later, she was asked to accompany her aunt to the Pump Room.

'Dear Maria is feeling a trifle delicate, so she will have to stay at home and rest,' Lady Marsh informed her. 'What with having to keep so many suitors at bay last night, it is not to be wondered at if she is tired, poor girl.'

Amelia hadn't noticed anyone showing any particular interest in her plain cousin, but didn't say so. As long as Lady Marsh believed it, she would be in a good mood and easier to deal with. Amelia went to fetch her bonnet and pelisse.

Bootle procured a chair for her ladyship, while Amelia was left to walk beside it. 'It is such a lovely spring day, after all, just right for some fresh air and exercise,' Lady Marsh declared. Amelia didn't protest, she walked along happily, revelling in the sights and sounds all around her. She thought Bath quite the most beautiful city she had ever seen, with its buildings of golden sandstone so neatly fitted on to the hillsides.

As they crossed Pulteney Bridge, she marvelled anew at its architecture and the beauty of the river flowing beneath it.

As soon as they entered the Pump Room, Lady Marsh spied some of her cronies and was soon ensconced with them, exchanging gossip about the previous night's ball. Amelia procured her a glass of the famous restorative water, then found herself dismissed. As she didn't know anyone, she wandered over to one of the tall windows overlooking the Roman pool, which had impressed her greatly the first time she saw it. She was not disappointed this time either; as it was such a cool day there was steam rising from the warm water to hang just above the surface in little clouds. This lent the whole aura of mystery that was quite breathtaking.

Her reverie was interrupted by a familiar voice.

'Please do not look at me, Miss Ravenscroft, then no-one will know that we are having a conversation.'

Amelia nodded almost imperceptibly and waited for Lord Demarr to continue. She gazed at the pool as if enraptured, but was in fact struggling to compose herself as the sound of his voice had made her jump.

'Good girl,' he said approvingly. 'I was going to send you word, but as you are here anyway... There has been a slight hitch in our plans. I have been unable to extricate myself from an engagement this evening without causing suspicions, so we will have to leave tomorrow night if you are agreeable?'

Again Amelia nodded slightly. 'Good. All the preparations are in hand and provided you can escape from the house undetected, there should be no reason for anyone to suspect that we have eloped.'

'Thank you,' Amelia breathed quietly. 'I was afraid you would have changed your mind this morning.' She chanced a glance in his direction, but this proved to be a mistake as her heart began to behave in a highly irregular manner when she saw him smile slightly.

'No, my dear, once I decide on something I never go back on my word. I will be there tomorrow night, never doubt it.'

'I'm glad.'

'I had best be off. I will get word to your butler when all is ready. Until then, au revoir.'

The next time Amelia glanced over to where he had stood, he was gone. She wondered if she was making the biggest mistake of her life, but surely nothing could be worse than staying in the same house as Bernard? She shuddered at the mere thought, and promptly returned to her aunt.

Much to Amelia's relief, Bernard took himself off soon after dinner, presumably to try and recoup his losses of the previous evening. She excused herself shortly after the tea tray had been removed and crawled gratefully into bed, falling asleep almost as soon as her head touched the pillow.

She was awakened suddenly just after midnight by someone placing a hand over her mouth, and her eyes flew open trying to see the intruder. She didn't really have to look, however.

As the odour of unwashed male and alcohol fumes reached her, she knew it couldn't be anyone other than Bernard. She saw him grinning at her in the faint moonlight in a very self-congratulatory way.

'Good evening, my dear cousin,' he whispered. 'I just thought I'd look in on you to see how you were sleeping.'

Amelia glanced at the door to see whether she had forgotten to lock it before she went to bed, although she didn't think so. He saw where she was looking and his grin broadened.

'No, you didn't forget to lock it, my sweet. I took the liberty of having a duplicate made this afternoon and it worked.' Triumphant, almost like a child who has gotten away with a naughty prank, he chuckled. A spoilt, selfish child was what he was, Amelia thought savagely, used to getting his own way. But not this time, she was determined on that.

She bit down hard on the hand that was still covering her mouth and he yelped and snatched it away. She spat out the taste of him and tried to roll away, but he was quicker and caught her arms, pinioning them to her sides.

'You little hellcat!' he exclaimed. 'I'll soon tame you.'

He proceeded to try to do just that, coming down heavily on top of her while he tried to kiss her. Amelia twisted and turned and bucked to heave him off, but when this did not succeed she tried to think of some other way. During their struggle, she managed to free one arm and groped around on her right table for something to hit him with. Nothing came to hand and she began to panic.

Suddenly, inspiration struck as she remembered something she had overheard one of the maids saying with a giggle to another. 'Kick 'im where it hurts the most,' she had said. Amelia decided it was worth a try, so she stopped struggling abruptly so that it would appear she had given up the fight. Bernard was pleased.

'That's better, sweet cousin, I've waited so long for ... aaaaggghh!'

Amelia's knee had connected with as much force as she could muster and Bernard reacted most satisfactorily. Cursing foully, he rolled off her, and in a flash Amelia was up and hunting for something else with which to disable him further.

Her fingers closed over the handle on the ewer on her washstand and without thinking, she lifted it up and brought it down on top of his head with a resounding crash. Bernard crumpled in a heap on the floor.

Amelia lit her candle with shaking hands, but almost dropped it as the door was flung open. It was only Bootle, however, and she drew a sigh of relief. 'Oh, thank God it's you!'

Bootle looked ready for a fight, but stopped short at the sight of Bernard. He allowed himself a small smile of satisfaction, before resuming his normally impassive expression. 'Ah, well done, Miss. I see you didn't need my assistance after all.'

'Oh, but I do. You must help me to carry him to his room.'

'It will be a pleasure.'

Before they had so much as lifted Bernard, however, Lady Marsh came rushing into the little room, pushing Bootle rudely out of the way and letting out a wail of distress at the sight of her son lying lifeless on the floor. She turned and slapped Amelia hard on the cheek.

'You ungrateful girl! Is this how you repay me for my kindness in taking you in when you were destitute? You should be ashamed of yourself. Bootle, remove Sir Bernard to his room, then go for the doctor at once. And as for you, you shall remain in this room until such time as I am ready to deal with you.'

She swept out majestically, leaving Bootle to struggle on his own with the dead weight of Bernard. 'I'll help you,' Amelia whispered, once Lady Marsh was out of earshot, and together they managed to carry her cousin to his bed. Before leaving him there, Amelia took the precaution of searching his pockets and found the duplicate key, which she gave to Bootle for safe-keeping.

She returned to her room, not worried in the least about either Bernard's condition or her aunt's threats. She was glad to have escaped the encounter with her virtue intact and shuddered at the thought of what might have happened. Automatically, she straightened the room, then returned to bed, but it was a long while before she managed to sleep again. She was more shaken by the attack than she cared to admit.

CHAPTER FOUR

The next day Amelia confided her plans to Bootle and although he was a bit doubtful at first, she soon convinced him that she was doing the right thing.

'I suppose marrying a Viscount, whoever he is, is better than becoming Sir Bernard's doxy,' he acknowledged. 'Though how you know you can trust the man, I'm not sure.'

Amelia was still worried about this herself, but she suppressed any doubts ruthlessly. She really couldn't stay in this house a moment longer and Lord Demarr had seemed sincere. Besides, if he reneged on their deal and tried the same tricks as Bernard, she was still no worse off.

Bootle fetched her a small valise, which was enough for her meagre possessions, and she spent the morning packing. Fortunately for her nerves, which were nearly at break-ing point, a message arrived shortly after lunchtime to say that she was to meet Lord Demarr at the entrance to the mews behind Lady Marsh's house at one o'clock in the morning. She prayed that all would be well.

The hours crept by unbelievably slowly, and Amelia thought the appointed time would never come. She dressed in a warm travelling dress of dark grey wool with a great many petticoats underneath, and put out a somewhat worn cloak to await her departure. When there was nothing left to do, she lay down on her bed fully clothed and waited.

Bootle tapped on her door at the appointed hour and took her valise as they tip-toed down the stairs. In order to reach the door to the back of the house, she had to traverse the landing on the first floor and go down to the front hall. One of the floorboards on the landing gave a loud creak and soon after a voice hissed at her from the shadows.

'And just where do you think you're going?' It was Maria, smiling maliciously in the moonlight. Amelia and Bootle stopped dead in their tracks.

'I am leaving this house,' she said with as much dignity as she could muster. 'I do not think I will be missed, do you?'

'Oh, but my dear brother would be most aggrieved to find you gone,' Maria purred. 'And let us not forget dear Mama. I feel sure she would have a thing or two to say to you that I wouldn't miss for the world.'

Amelia frowned, frustrated beyond belief. 'So what are you going to do, carry me upstairs?'

'I don't think there's any need for that. I shall just scream.'

Amelia had never felt so much like hitting someone in her entire life and wondered if there was something about this household that brought out a violent streak in her. There was nothing for it but to turn round, however, and Maria glided behind her like a malicious ghost in her white nightdress. As soon as Amelia had entered her room again, Maria turned the key in the lock from the outside with a low laugh.

'Sleep well, dear cousin, I look forward to seeing you in the morning.'

Amelia began to pace the floor and wondered what on earth to do now. She would have to hope that Bootle could sneak back upstairs when Maria had gone to sleep, but that might be hours from now and then Lord Demarr would be gone. She looked wistfully out into the garden, which seemed very far down. Even if she tied all her sheets together, she would never be able to reach it.

She had just about given up all hope, when suddenly she spied movement in the garden. A small thud was heard against the outside wall, and when she opened her window to see what was going on she saw a figure climbing up towards her on a ladder. She recognised Lord Demarr and her heart lodged somewhere near her throat. He was taking an awful risk. What if Bernard, whose room was towards the back, should wake up and see him?

Lord Demarr was now at the top of the

ladder, but it didn't quite reach Amelia's window. 'You must tie up your sheets,' he whispered, 'and slide down to me. Hurry if you wish to escape from here.'

Amelia nodded. This was no time to be missish and she hurried to do his bidding. First she lowered her valise down to him and waited while he took it to the ground, then she did as she had been told. He guided her feet towards the rung of the ladder and helped to steady her from behind.

As she felt one of his hands around her waist, she breathed a sigh of relief and a feeling of security spread through her. She was filled with exhilaration, as if she was setting out on an adventure, which indeed she was.

Safely on the ground, the Viscount steadied her and whispered, 'Good girl, I knew you could do it. Now let's be on our way.'

Bootle took away the ladder as quietly as possible, while the others crept into the mews behind the house and along to the waiting carriage. Bootle came hurrying behind them with the valise, which Lord Demarr gave to one of the positions. The butler was looking a trifle anxious, but his lordship reassured him.

'Don't worry, my good man, Miss Ravenscroft will not come to any harm with me.'

'Good luck and godspeed, Miss Amelia,' Bootle whispered and on impulse Amelia flung her arms around him for a quick embrace.

'Thank you, Bootle, you have been a great help. If there is ever anything I can do for you...'

'Yes, indeed,' Lord Demarr added. 'Do come to us if there is any trouble for you here. But now we must away.'

Amelia leaned back on to the softly cushioned seat and looked around her with interest. Despite the darkness, she could see that it was a beautifully appointed carriage, the interior done up in velvet. It was also well-sprung and comfortable, she was hardly bounced around at all.

'I must thank you for coming to my rescue,

my lord,' she said, feeling rather nervous now that they were alone together in the dark carriage.

'It was nothing. Bootle came to find me and told me what had occurred and I thought it best to get you out as soon as possible. I have to say it made me very angry indeed that they should blame you for defending yourself from that lecher, not to mention his sister conniving at it as well.'

He looked almost savage as he said this, and Amelia thought to herself that she wouldn't like to be on the receiving end of his wrath. She decided a change of subject might be in order.

'Is this your carriage, my lord?'

'No, I decided to hire one as we didn't want to advertise our intentions. My own carriage has my arms blazoned on the side, so I sent it home with some of my luggage. Hopefully people will think I returned with it.'

'Good idea. And I left a note saying I was going to London to seek employment. No-one even knows we are acquainted, so hopefully they won't connect the two.'

The Viscount gave her an enigmatic look, then smiled slightly. 'No, we're not really acquainted, are we. Perhaps we should pass the time by rectifying that matter?'

'Wha-what do you mean?' Amelia stammered, wondering again what she had let herself in for. Was he suggesting they jump their marriage vows?

He smiled again. 'I only meant that perhaps we should talk to each other and find out about our likes and dislikes and so on. See if we have any mutual interests?'

'Oh, yes, of course.' Amelia felt very foolish. 'I'm sorry, I seem to be a little jumpy today and after what happened last night...'

'Well, I can assure you I am not an ogre. You are safe with me.'

James still felt anger swirl inside him as he saw the anxiousness in Amelia's eyes. He would have liked to go back and wring Sir Bernard's neck, but he contented himself with the thought that the man's plans had been foiled and he had come by his just desserts. He hoped he had a very sore head indeed.

'It was very resourceful of you, my dear, to hit Sir Bernard with the ewer,' he said. 'I hope you don't intend to treat me like that?' he added jokingly.

'Oh, no.' Amelia smiled, relaxing a little at last. 'Besides, now you are forewarned of my little tricks, you will be able to guard against them. Poor Bernard was a totally unsuspecting victim.' She began to laugh. 'You should have seen his face?'

'His face?'

'How surprised he looked. He was so convinced I would eventually welcome him with open arms, it never occurred to him that he wouldn't prevail.'

James joined in the laughter. 'Indeed. Men such as he believe they have a right to behave as they wish. Thank goodness you disabused him of that notion.'

They spent the next few hours talking, sharing anecdotes about their families and learning about each other. Surprisingly, they found that they liked the same kind of music, art and literature, and they had a lengthy discussion on each of these subjects. James was astonished at her extensive knowledge.

'How come you are so well versed in all these subjects?' he asked.

'I was my father's only child and I think that because he had wished for a boy, he more or less treated me as one.'

James thought this strange, but had to acknowledge that it was good to be able to talk to her as an equal.

She didn't seem bored by any topic, not even farming, which was something he had taken an interest in recently, and she was even able to add to his knowledge occasionally.

Finally, the long hours of worry took their toll on Amelia, and her eyelids began to droop.

'Here, you may lean against my shoulder,' he invited. 'Go to sleep and I will wake you when it is time for breakfast.'

She was inclined to argue at first, but she was too tired to keep it up and eventually succumbed to slumber. James put his arm around her and simply held her, a strange feeling of protectiveness filling him. He wondered at it, but it felt good, so he simply closed his own eyes and went to sleep.

They travelled all night, heading north through the Cotswolds, and stopped only once to change the horses. They passed by Cheltenham, James preferring to stop at smaller towns so as to put anyone following them off the scent.

Finally, they came to a halt at a country inn late in the morning and he shook Amelia gently to wake her up.

'Time for some breakfast, or perhaps lunch? I've asked for a private parlour.'

'Thank you, that would be wonderful.' Amelia followed him into the inn. She felt slightly flustered when the landlady addressed her as 'her ladyship', but James sent her a warning glance and she played along with this. He had said he thought it best that they pose as a married couple.

Their ruse brought it home to her more forcibly just what she was doing – eloping with a complete stranger who could be a wanted man for all she knew. The tension of the previous day returned as she wondered whether Bernard was even now on their trail, thundering north to stop this marriage. And what of her aunt?

By now she would have read the note Amelia left, and no doubt was in a fearful temper at having lost her unpaid servant. Amelia shivered involuntarily and took a deep breath. She must stop thinking about it and hope for the best.

In order to calm down, she went to freshen up and when she returned, James was already seated at a table groaning with food, looking for all the world as if this was just a normal day. Amelia decided to follow his lead, there was no point in worrying now, the die was cast. She sat down and joined him, tucking in with gusto. She had always had a hearty appetite, even when under pressure.

'You do not seem to subscribe to the popular idea that young ladies should eat virtually nothing,' he commented, glancing unobtrusively at her waistline. 'Although I must say, I prefer ladies who don't look as though they would blow away in a gust of wind,' he added, obviously anxious not to insult her.

Amelia only smiled and replied airily, 'Oh, I like to eat a lot at breakfast time to sustain me through the day, but then I usually take a lot of exercise one way or another.' She had forgotten that she was still wearing the padding, but there seemed no point in discarding it yet. After all, if James married her looking like this, she could be sure he wasn't as shallow as Bernard.

James hid a frown and privately doubted whether the exercise Amelia claimed to take was enough, judging by her plump figure, but he was too polite to say so. And he had not chosen her for her looks after all, or had he?

He looked at her again, observing the pretty face with hyacinth blue eyes that sparkled in the morning light. Her hair was still dreadful, but perhaps with a little help from a hairdresser she could be quite presentable. He shook himself mentally. What did it matter?

They were soon on their way again and time passed quickly in conversation. Amelia was eager to hear everything James could tell her about the places they were passing through, and he found himself regarding everything through her enthusiastic eyes.

Sometimes they simply sat in companionable silence, but it was not strained in any way and James surprised himself by thinking that he had seldom felt so at ease with anyone before. It was as if they had known each other for a long time and he wondered why this was so.

They stayed the night at another small country inn, where the innkeeper was honoured enough by such exalted guests to give them his best two bedchambers. Amelia worried all through dinner about the sleeping arrangements, as their rooms were connected, but to her relief his lordship simply bade her goodnight outside her door and said, 'I'll see you in the morning.' She was very grateful that he hadn't made any demands on her as yet.

The following morning she took the liberty of ordering a bath and had a long soak before washing her hair. It was wonderful to have clean hair again, and she revelled in the silky feel of it as she combed it out. Keeping it dirty and in an unflattering style had been one of the subterfuges she had employed in order to possibly put Bernard off, although sadly that had not worked for any length of time.

When her hair was reasonably dry, she put it up in a simple knot on the top of her head, and was pleased at the effect this had on the Viscount when she descended for breakfast.

'I say, that hairstyle becomes you very well,' he exclaimed. Amelia turned away to hide a smile. She had seen him eyeing her ringlets with disgust and she couldn't blame him, they had been dreadful indeed.

'Thank you, my lord.'

They continued their journey and made good time. There was no sign of anyone following them, and Amelia began to relax and enjoy herself. They stopped overnight again and in the afternoon of the following day they finally approached the border of Scotland.

As they drew nearer to their destination, Amelia once again became a trifle nervous. After all, she was marrying a virtual stranger in far from normal circumstances and she didn't know what the future would hold. However, she was of an optimistic nature and would not let herself dwell too much on unpleasant possibilities. It was therefore with a cheerful smile that she later entered the forge at Gretna Green.

His lordship looked as handsome as ever, and Amelia felt a jolt of awareness stab her. He gave her a small smile and handed her a bouquet of flowers with a flourish. 'For the bride,' he said.

'Why, thank you! How thoughtful,' she

murmured, almost overcome by this kind gesture. Any doubts she may have been harbouring fled in that moment. She was marrying a nice, kind man and she was doing the right thing.

The ceremony was luckily very brief and after they had signed the register, they went back to their inn for an early dinner. Amelia felt quite exhausted from the journey and all that had happened beforehand, but she knew that tonight there would be no sleep for her until after she had fulfilled all her wifely obligations. Although she did know what these duties entailed, she was understandably nervous and sat picking at her dinner.

'You are not hungry?' his lordship enquired.

'Yes, I mean no. I'm just a little tired.' She felt herself blushing under his scrutiny and stared at her plate.

'You are not afraid of me, are you?' he asked gently. 'I assure you I would never hurt you in any way.'

'Oh, no. Of course not, my lord.'

'Perhaps you could call me James now that we are married, Amelia?'

'I … yes, if you wish, er, James.'

He handed her a glass of wine. 'Here, a drink of this will calm your nerves.'

Amelia accepted gratefully and drank deeply, forgetting that she hadn't eaten very much. The wine went to her head very quickly and she began to feel much more composed and cheerful. So much so, that the meal passed in a blur and before she knew it, she had consumed at least three glasses of wine, with the result that she felt a bit strange when she stood up.

James did not seem to notice, however, and simply picked her up and carried her to his chamber, where he put her down just in front of him. A frisson slithered through Amelia as her body came into contact with his, and when he put his arms around her it felt so right.

She twined her arms around his neck with a smile and when he bent to kiss her, it was even more wonderful than the first time on the terrace, and she responded eagerly.

He kissed her slowly at first, almost reverently, then began to deepen the kiss. The most wonderful sensations began to course through her and it was beyond anything she had ever felt in her life. Eagerly, she pulled him closer to kiss him back in equal measure, but her passionate response was suddenly cut short, as James tore his mouth away and held her at arm's length, staring at her with a frown.

'What's wrong?' she asked, confused and dizzy.

'I think perhaps we need more time to get to know each other before we pursue this, my dear,' he said. His voice sounded oddly cold and Amelia shivered. Had she put him off with her ardour she wondered.

She knew that young ladies of quality were not supposed to show their feelings, but she had not thought this applied to encounters with one's own husband.

'As you wish,' she murmured, distraught that she may have given him a disgust of her. She stumbled towards the bed and sat down abruptly.

'It would be best if we get a good night's sleep, we have much to do tomorrow,' James said and went over to his side of the bed.

Engulfed in misery, Amelia hardly noticed as he blew out the candles, undressed and lay down. Without looking at him, she did the same in the dark, but it was a long time before sleep claimed her.

James lay staring into the darkness, very aware of the woman only a few feet away from him. The woman who had been willing to give him everything she had to offer.

He had wanted her – still wanted her – with a fierceness that had taken him by surprise, but her passionate response to his kiss had made warning bells ring inside his brain and stopped him from taking things further. He found himself wondering how much he really knew about his new wife – what if she were not the innocent she claimed to be? What if he had been duped and she really had been Sir Bernard's mistress already?

Perhaps this was all a ruse so that Sir Bernard would not have to accept the consequences of his actions? What if Amelia was already with child? She had claimed not to be, but she could have been lying.

A cold knot formed in his stomach. He would have looked a fool indeed if she was pregnant and he had to claim the child as his own simply because he couldn't wait to bed her himself. It would account for her willingness to marry a man she barely knew and her wanton behaviour just now.

James began to think of more and more possibilities, his mind torturing him with visions of Amelia kissing someone else as passionately as she had him. All the conversations they had had during the journey, when he had begun to like and trust her, were instantly forgotten.

I must have been mad, he thought. I should have checked her story more thoroughly. But he had been taken in by her air of a damsel in distress and the loathsome Sir Bernard had certainly done his bit to convince him.

James swore silently. Well, he would not fall for her wiles. If she was with child, let her try and foist it on someone else. He would bide his time and make sure before he touched her again. Until then, she would be his wife in name only.

James was already gone by the time Amelia was awakened by a kindly maid-servant who brought her hot water to wash with and some breakfast.

Amelia's head was throbbing with the after effects of the wine, but she made herself eat a little nonetheless. James had said they had a busy day ahead of them, so she needed something to settle her stomach.

Just as she had finished eating, her new husband entered the room, looking as if nothing had happened at all. Amelia frowned slightly, but could not pluck up the courage to ask him anything about it.

'Are you ready?' he asked. 'We are going to Carlisle to buy you some clothes. I can't arrive home with a wife who is dressed in cast-offs, which is what I take that to be?' He nodded towards the dress she was wearing, which was indeed one that had belonged to Lady Marsh. 'And I did promise to buy you a new wardrobe, did I not?'

'Yes, I remember you mentioning it, but I'm sure just a few things will do for now.'

'We'll see,' was all he would say before hurrying her out of the room.

Carlisle was not very far from Gretna Green and they found it to be quite a large bustling place. After making enquiries, they were directed to a dressmaker in the High Street who, although very obviously not of French origin, called herself Madame Antoinette. After having met the lady, Amelia hoped quietly to herself that the lady's talent for dressmaking was rather better than her acting skills as her French accent was atrocious. Fortunately this soon proved to be the case.

Madame ushered Amelia into a changing room and ordered her to take off her clothes. Amelia obeyed and waited for the exclamation she knew was coming.

'Oh, la, la! What on earth? Why are you wearing zat?' Madame Antoinette pointed to the roll of padding around Amelia's waist. 'Are you mad, my lady? I mean, I beg your pardon, but who in zeir right mind wants to be fatter zan zey have to?'

Amelia smiled. 'I was trying to make myself unattractive in order to keep a suitor at bay,' she explained, 'but I suppose I no longer need it now.'

'Well, no more! Off, off with it I say.' Madame wasn't having any of this. 'You have a lovely figure, we must show it off to ze Monsieur. Oui, oui.'

It was therefore a rather svelte Amelia who emerged dressed in a gown Madame had made for someone else who now no longer wanted it. It was a low-cut evening dress of ice blue satin with an overdress of silver gauze, and Amelia felt distinctly uncomfortable with so much of her bosom on display, but it was a beautiful dress and she had to admit that it fitted her perfectly.

James, who had been idly flicking through

a book of prints while sipping a glass of wine, looked up and almost choked on his latest mouthful.

'What the devil…? What have you done to yourself?' He stood up abruptly and came over to inspect her more closely. 'I won't have you squeezing yourself into corsets in the name of fashion. That's ridiculous. You will surely faint.'

'I'm not wearing a corset, James, I … well, it's a long story. You see, I was wearing padding to make myself appear slightly larger than I really am.'

'Whatever for?' He was scowling at her and she took a step back.

'To put Bernard off, although it didn't work very well. So what do you think? Will this gown do?'

James still looked flummoxed and didn't reply immediately. He looked very annoyed indeed, and Amelia couldn't understand why her subterfuge should rile him so. She put a hand on his arm and said, 'I'm sorry if I've startled you, I suppose I should have removed the padding before, but I was just so used to it, I forgot.'

He snatched his arm away as if she had branded him, and Amelia couldn't help but feel hurt that her touch affected him thus. If he couldn't bear for her to even put a hand on his arm, how would they ever live together? She turned around, with drooping shoulders, and muttered something about trying on another gown.

James stared after her as she disappeared behind the curtain yet again. He could not but see her pretence as yet another instance of her having duped him. He supposed he should have noticed when he held her in his arms the night before, but he had been so intent on kissing her, it never occurred to him that her waist felt strange.

He ought to be grateful that she was so much prettier than he had thought. Her bosom had not been faked, and combined with the narrow waist it gave her a stunning figure. Still, he couldn't shake the feeling that she was taking him for a ride, and it was not one he relished.

He had married a deceitful woman or was he wrong about her? He wished he knew.

Amelia had lost all her enthusiasm for clothes shopping, but Madame was nothing if not thorough. Amelia soon found herself the owner of several morning dresses, two evening gowns, a ball gown, a carriage dress and no less than three walking dresses. There was also an array of underwear and every other item a lady could possibly require, including a lovely fur-trimmed travelling cloak, a small Spencer jacket and a short silk pelisse. James further insisted that she should have a riding outfit.

'You are, after all, going to live in the country most of the time,' he said, and added as an afterthought. 'You do ride, I take it?'

'Yes, of course I do,' Amelia answered, exasperated with his strange mood. 'My father saw to it that I had the best possible tuition.'

On the way back to the inn, they stopped at a milliner to acquire several different bonnets to match her new outfits, and they also bought some new boots, slippers and gloves. Amelia's head fairly whirled with it all and she wondered vaguely if they would have to hire an extra carriage just to bring all her luggage.

'It was lucky that Madame Antoinette had so many gowns already made up,' James commented on the way back to the inn.

'Yes, she said they were for some young woman whose mother died before she was able to go off on her season. How very sad.'

'But fortunate for us.'

'Indeed. Thank you very much for buying me all those things, you have been far too generous. I'm sure I didn't need the half of it.'

'It was nothing. I can't have my wife looking like a dowd,' he replied, looking so forbidding Amelia didn't dare pursue the topic. She didn't yet know enough about her new husband to be able to coax him out of his bad humour, so she could only wait and hope that it would pass.

CHAPTER FIVE

They began their journey south the following morning, but it was very different from the one they had shared before. James said hardly a word and Amelia did not dare initiate any conversations when he looked so stern. Consequently, they travelled in silence most of the time and Amelia found that she missed the companionship they had shared on the way north.

If she was perfectly honest with herself, she had begun to like James very much during those conversations, and even though he had been acting strange since the wedding, she still found him attractive. Just sitting in the same carriage as him did funny things to her insides, and whenever his gaze rested on her, she felt warm all over. She could only hope that his mood would improve soon so that they could continue to get to know each other.

The southward journey was accomplished at a slightly slower pace and they stopped overnight several times.

'Your two best chambers, if you please,' James demanded each time, and Amelia didn't know whether to be grateful or sorry that they slept in separate rooms every night.

During a rare exchange of conversation, he told her that they needed to stop in London to sort out all the legalities of their marriage with his lawyers, but there was no point opening up his town house for just one night.

'You won't mind staying at Brown's Hotel, will you?' he asked.

'No, of course not.' Brown's was considered one of the finest in London, how could she possibly object, Amelia wondered.

Their suite consisted of two bedrooms with a shared sitting room in between, and it was done up in the best possible taste. There were some surprised glances from the staff when James demanded the use of a maid for his wife, but he lied glibly telling them that her own maid had been taken ill during the journey and had to be left behind. A nice cheerful girl soon arrived to assist Amelia with changing her gown and arranging her hair.

After a quick luncheon, served in their private sitting room, they went off to pay a visit to his lawyers, whose offices were situated near the Inns of Court. They were ushered into the office of a Mr Jarvis almost immediately, and he proved to be a small wiry man with glasses, behind which were a pair of very sharp eyes that seemed to miss nothing.

'Lord Demarr, what a pleasure to see you again.'

'Indeed, Mr Jarvis, I trust we find you well?' James indicated Amelia and said, 'May I introduce my wife, Lady Demarr, formerly Miss Amelia Ravenscroft.'

'Lady Demarr, how do you do?' Mr Jarvis bowed over her hand politely. 'But how is this? I have not seen any announcements in the papers.' Amelia felt sure he would never have missed something so important and smiled inwardly.

'No, I'm afraid we have been very remiss in that quarter,' James replied as he handed Amelia into a chair and sat down himself. 'You see, we have only been married a week and I'm afraid it was a somewhat clandestine affair. Gretna Green, in fact. For reasons we will not go into now, my wife's guardian would not have approved our marriage.'

'I see. May I see the marriage lines, my lord?'

'Of course.' James handed him the papers. 'I would be grateful if you would keep them here, somewhere very safe. I wouldn't like them to fall into the wrong hands.'

'Naturally.' Mr Jarvis took his request in his stride. 'And do I take it you wish to draw up some settlements?'

'That's right.'

There followed a lengthy session which Amelia gave up trying to follow after a while.

She was only called upon to give her own details, and when she mentioned her father's name, Mr Jarvis muttered, 'Excellent family that,' which pleased her.

When all was complete and signed, James explained to her that for now, she would have a monthly allowance to enable her to buy whatever she needed, and in the event of his death she would be given a handsome jointure and a dower house, while the rest of his estate would be divided between his children. 'Does that seem fair?'

'You have been more than generous, thank you.' Amelia almost felt guilty for accepting and tried to thank him again on the way back to the hotel.

'It is nothing. I am not a poor man and I would not have it said that I was ever stingy towards my wife.'

Upon their return to the hotel, James surprised her by suggesting a visit to the opera that evening, in order to pass the time. Amelia accepted with alacrity, as she had a passion for the opera and indeed had an excellent singing voice herself. Her father had often bemoaned the fact that she could not show off her own talent in Covent Garden, but instead he had made her give private recitals to their friends, which were much sought after.

Dressed in her new ice blue evening gown, Amelia sat down in the box James had procured with barely concealed excitement and prepared to enjoy herself. She glanced at her handsome husband from time to time, and despite the fact that no one openly acknowledged them, there were many people who stared at them from behind their fans or studied them covertly. Amelia pretended as if they didn't exist.

'You don't mind the old biddies staring down their noses at you?' James whispered.

'Not at all. I told you I wouldn't mind being ostracised, and I meant it. Those people are nothing to me.'

'That's my girl,' he said with an approving smile.

During the first pause they were promenading together in the corridor, amicably discussing the performance so far, when to their surprise a distinguished military man in his early thirties, with a rakish mane of russet hair and a dashing moustache, stopped in front of them and hailed Amelia loudly.

'Miss Ravenscroft, by all that's holy! I never thought to see you here. What a fortunate coincidence, we have all been wondering what had become of you. Haven't seen hide nor hair of you since the sad day of your father's funeral.'

'Captain Marshall, how nice to see you again,' Amelia was astonished to meet someone she knew, but recovered her composure quickly. 'I am very well, thank you. Permit me to introduce my husband, Lord Demarr. James, this is Captain Marshall, a friend of my late father's and a member of his regiment.'

'Delighted, I'm sure,' James replied, but his expression didn't match his words, which puzzled Amelia.

'You must forgive me,' Captain Marshall

said. 'I had not heard of your marriage. My congratulations to both of you. I do hope you appreciate your wife's talents as much as the rest of us did, my dear fellow. She's a capital girl,' he added in an aside to James, following this with a large booming laugh.

James scowled and sent Amelia an enquiring glance. She blushed and stammered. 'Oh, I'm sure my talents are nothing to equal the ladies of Covent Garden, Captain.'

'Nonsense, I'm sure you reduced a few of my men to tears.' The Captain laughed again. 'Did she tell you, my lord, that we used to call her the "Silver Nightingale"?'

'No, she didn't. And now if you will excuse us, we really must return to our box.' James had an almost murderous look on his face, Amelia noted with a sinking feeling, and wondered why her talent for singing should have made him so angry.

'Hope to see you soon again,' the Captain called after them cheerfully.

Amelia was virtually frog-marched back to their box and by the time they reached it she was feeling very ill-used.

'Is it a crime to have acquaintances?' she asked sarcastically.

'That depends on how well acquainted you are,' James bit back. 'Let us watch the rest of the opera, we will discuss this later.'

The music had lost its enchantment for Amelia, however, and she counted the minutes until it was time to leave. She couldn't understand what had got into James, but she was determined to find out as soon as they were back at the hotel.

James sat silently fuming all through the second act and couldn't wait to get back either. He wanted to know precisely what 'talent' had caused other men to give his wife a nickname, and he wanted to know who all these other men were. His worries ate into him so that by the time they finally reached the hotel, he had worked himself into a towering rage.

The moment they stepped into the foyer, he took his wife by the arm and virtually dragged her into a small side room, which happened to house an assortment of instruments. He ignored them and turned to confront her, but she yanked her arm free and spoke first.

'What on earth is the matter with you?' she hissed furiously. 'If I'm not allowed to speak to people in public other than yourself, you should have told me beforehand, not treat me like some common doxy you can drag around any way you please.'

'And what if that's exactly what you are, madam?' he shot back.

'How dare you?' Her hand shot out to hit him on the cheek, but he caught it easily, infuriating her even further.

'Not so fast, my dear. First I would like to know who all these people are who didn't know "where you had disappeared to" and second of all, I would like an explanation of your so called talent.'

'The people in question were my father's military colleagues. I told you, we used to entertain the officers from a nearby army headquarters from time to time. Those were the people he gambled with too. Some of them were married and often brought their wives. As for my "talent", I sing a little, that's all. Occasionally I used to entertain my father's friends.'

'I bet you did.'

'If you are going to be rude, I'm going to bed.'

'Your talent must be quite considerable if it earned you a nickname. Show me.'

'What here? Now? Are you mad?' Amelia was acutely conscious of all the other people in the hotel lobby and had no wish to make a spectacle of herself.

'Why not? Everyone else seems to have heard you perform, why not your husband?'

'Whatever would the other guests say? It's very late.' Amelia glanced at the half-open door. She knew that her voice would carry far beyond this room if she gave it full rein.

'I don't give a damn,' James exploded. 'Just sing!'

Fury gave Amelia the courage to do as he asked. 'Very well, but if we are thrown out of here, it will be your fault.'

She sat down at the pianoforte that stood in the middle of the room and began to strum a few notes softly, while she collected herself and decided what to sing. She was out of practice and hadn't sung for a while, so she decided on something simple and chose one of the lesser arias from the opera they had just seen. She knew it by heart and once she began to sing, albeit haltingly at first, she soon forgot where she was and lost herself in the music.

Her voice gained confidence, and rang out sweet and pure, and towards the end of the aria she sang with all her might. By the time she had finished, a crowd had gathered in the doorway and everyone began to clap enthusiastically. James said nothing, just offered her his arm as she stood up and prepared to leave.

She swept past him, however, still angry, but smiled mechanically to acknowledge the applause, then she went straight up to her room, slamming the door behind her.

If he was going to be this dictatorial, how on earth was their marriage going to work? One thing was for sure, she would not put up with it.

CHAPTER SIX

James was in a quandary. He had a feeling he had just made a great fool of himself and it was not a feeling he relished. His wife had proved to him that she did indeed possess a rare talent, in fact, he would not be surprised if she had reduced grown men to tears with a voice like that, but it still rankled that she had sung to other men, married or otherwise. He was beginning to wonder why that should matter to him so much.

It would seem he was jealous, but how could that be? Being jealous meant that he would first have to be in love, and he refused to acknowledge any such thing. He didn't even dare believe in Amelia's innocence, so he couldn't possibly love her. Or could he?

No. He decided that without trust there could be no love. He had to be sure and what was needed was a breathing space, some time for reflection. Everything had happened with such speed, they had to slow things down a little. The best thing would be for him to leave Amelia at his home in Surrey for a few weeks while he attended to some of his other properties.

Perhaps after some time away from her he could begin to think clearly again. He had found that being with her played havoc with his senses and his brain didn't seem to function like it normally did. He had to get away.

When Amelia woke the next morning, James had already gone out.

'Said as how he had some business to take care of,' the maid informed her.

Amelia wondered what to do while she waited for him and decided she had better just stay in the hotel. She had no idea why James had acted so strangely the night before, but during the night she had calmed down and come to the conclusion that it had probably all been a misunderstanding. She really needed to be patient until she learned more about him. They were, after all, virtually strangers still, and no doubt she would understand him better once they got to know each other properly.

She went downstairs to look for a periodical with which to pass the time, and sat down in the lounge by herself. She had just finished the first page when a footman came over to her with a card on a silver salver.

'There's a gentleman who'd like a word with you, my lady.'

Amelia looked at the card, which bore the name of Captain Marshall, and groaned inwardly. She wasn't sure she ought to see him without James being present, but on the other hand she was sitting in a room full of people so there couldn't be any impropriety in simply talking to the man.

'Very well, show him over here, please,' she said to the footman.

Soon after, the captain's booming voice rang out. 'Lady Demarr, how do you do?' He bowed over her hand, but she snatched it back as quickly as possible.

'How nice of you to call, please take a seat,' she said. 'How did you know where to find me?'

'Oh, we military chaps have connections, you know.'

'I see. Well, what can I do for you?'

'Nothing, m'dear, nothing. It's the other way around, actually, I came to ask if there was anything I could help you with?'

'Me? No, really I'm fine.' Amelia was confused by his offer, but didn't know what to say.

Captain Marshall looked around furtively, then bent forward to whisper theatrically, 'Just thought I'd come and ask, you know. Your husband didn't seem to be in a very good mood last night. Not treating you badly, is he? Be honoured to take care of him for you if he was.' He nodded for emphasis.

Amelia was aghast. The last thing she

needed at the moment was some other man championing her cause. She didn't think James would like that at all.

'No, Captain,' she said firmly, 'everything is fine, I assure you. No-one could ask for a better husband, truly.' She tried to look as sincere as possible and evidently succeeded since the captain looked satisfied.

'Just thought I'd make sure, m'dear. Owe it to your father to look out for you.'

'Thank you, it's very kind, but there is no need. I'm very happy with my marriage.'

'And I'm very happy to hear that,' a new voice entered the conversation and Amelia felt her spirits sink. James. Why did he have to arrive now of all times?

'The Captain was just leaving,' she said nervously. She looked at James to see what his reaction had been, then rather wished she hadn't. His face was set in a very forbidding expression, his icy gaze on the Captain, who swiftly took his leave.

'Shall we take lunch in our room, madam?' James asked, still icily polite.

'Yes, of course.' Amelia wondered if it was her fate to be forever in disgrace, but she didn't see how she could have avoided talking to the captain. When they reached their room, James turned on her at once.

'Can I not leave you for five minutes without finding you smiling at some gentleman? I do not expect to find my wife sitting in the common lounge talking to someone, is that understood?'

'Perfectly. Should I have asked the Captain up to our sitting-room then, where I was without a chaperone?'

'I do not want you to entertain gentlemen callers at all,' he fairly shouted. 'Perhaps you need a little reminder as to who your husband is?' And without warning, he took her in his arms and began to kiss her ruthlessly.

Amelia had no doubt it was meant as a punishment, but she could not help her enjoyment of the kiss and soon responded in kind, thus unwittingly beating him at his own game. He broke it off looking thoroughly frustrated.

'I think in the circumstances it would be best if we set off for my country estate immediately. If you would be so good as to pack?'

He stalked off towards his room and slammed the door, leaving Amelia feeling exasperated once again. What an infuriating and difficult man he was, she thought, but so attractive at the same time. She sighed. Would she ever understand him?

The last leg of their journey was accomplished in stony silence. Amelia knew where they were going, since James had told her previously that his home was near East Grinstead, but she had no idea how long it would take to get there. She refused to ask though.

It didn't take more than half a day, in fact, and when they arrived Amelia couldn't help but exclaim in surprise. He had said that he owned a 'small property,' and Amelia hadn't much cared about the size of her prospective new home, but what lay before her was nothing less than a mansion. As the carriage swept through a well-kept park, a beautiful house in the Palladian style came into view, with neatly laid-out formal gardens all around it.

'This is Marr Place?' she asked incredulously, and James, obviously pleased with her reaction, unbent enough to reply.

'Indeed. Do you like it?'

'Like it? It's magnificent! I thought you said you had a small property.'

'Well, it's small in comparison to some. My grandfather's house is much larger.'

Amelia did not reply, but stared at the house instead. She couldn't believe she was going to be the mistress of such a grand establishment. It was too good to be true, but also daunting in the extreme. What if she couldn't manage such a large household? She shook herself mentally and told herself sternly not to be so silly.

The carriage came to a halt next to a curving flight of steps leading up to the front portico. As James helped her alight, Amelia marvelled anew at the beauty of the house, but her attention was soon claimed by the front door opening, and a butler who greeted them with a bow.

'Ah, Jamieson, forgive our sudden arrival, but we finished our business in town a trifle early,' James said to the butler. 'I'm sure that with your usual efficiency you have already arranged everything to our satisfaction.'

'Indeed, my lord. We have been ready for days. May I take this opportunity to wish you joy and on behalf of myself and all the staff to welcome her ladyship to her new home.'

'Thank you.' Amelia smiled at him. 'You are very kind.'

Next, she was introduced to the house-keeper, Mrs Flint, and this lady escorted her upstairs to her room, which proved to be an entire suite on the second floor overlooking the park. It was decorated in shades of moss green and gold and Amelia could not but approve of this choice as green was one of her favourite colours.

'This is lovely!' she exclaimed.

Mrs Flint looked pleased, but said, 'To be sure, we hope you will find everything satis-factory, although I expect you'll want to make some changes.'

'Oh no, not in here at any rate. This is just perfect.'

'I'm glad you like it, my lady. Now I will send up one of the maids to help you with your unpacking. Her name is Maryann and if you approve of her, she can be your maid, as I understand from his lordship's letter that you didn't bring anyone with you.' There was a knock on the door. 'Ah, here she is now with some hot water and towels.'

'Thank you, Mrs Flint, you have thought of everything.'

Amelia was soon pleased to approve the housekeeper's choice of maid for her, as Maryann was a very capable country girl, cheerful and willing to help. Together they set about repairing the ravages of the journey.

CHAPTER SEVEN

Amelia was asked to join his lordship in the library as soon as she was finished, and with a last look in the mirror she followed a footman downstairs. She felt unaccountably nervous, despite knowing that she looked her best in one of her new gowns, and wondered what mood James would be in now.

The library proved to be very grand, its walls covered with bookcases from floor to ceiling, with little niches in between which housed tiny antique marble statues. The high ceiling was covered in lavish plaster decorations and the windows were draped in burgundy velvet, a colour scheme echoed in the furnishings and thick Oriental carpet. The footman announced her, then bowed and took his leave.

James watched her as she approached, then

indicated that she should take a seat near the fireplace. He took the chair opposite.

'I have been doing a lot of thinking since yesterday evening,' he began, 'and I have decided that perhaps we need some time away from each other to enable us to get used to this strange bargain we have struck. I own a stud farm not far from here called Westfield, and I propose to go and stay there for a while. It is no great distance, so you can contact me at any time if necessary.'

Amelia was taken aback. 'I see,' she said calmly, although inwardly she wanted to rail at him. They had made a bargain, that much was true, but surely it would be better for them to live together if they wanted to get used to it? She said nothing, however, merely asked if she could be in charge of the household while he was gone.

'Yes, of course, and you may do as you please. This is your home now, and if you wish to have it redecorated from top to bottom, you are free to do so. I leave it entirely up to you and should you need funds for anything, just send a groom over to me with a note. I think you will find that the shop-keepers in these parts will be only too happy to extend you credit and send their bills to me.'

'Very well. Thank you.' Amelia didn't know what else to say, so she folded her hands in her lap and waited.

'There is one more thing,' James said. 'I have asked the children's nanny to bring them down here to be introduced to you. Perhaps you can oblige me by becoming acquainted with them while I am away?'

As he finished speaking, there was a knock on the door and upon his 'Enter,' a rather sour-faced woman in her early thirties came in with two little girls in tow.

'Ah, there you are, Miss Downes, children. Amelia, allow me to present my daughters, Mathilde, who is six, and Chloe, who is four. This is their nanny, Miss Downes. Girls, this is your new step-mama, my wife. Please come and make your curtseys.'

He sounded stern and Amelia was just

beginning to wonder what sort of man she had married, when he added with a smile, 'And then you may come and give your papa a kiss.'

The little girls obediently curtseyed to Amelia, under the watchful eye of the nanny, but only the older one said, 'Pleased to meet you, ma'am.' She was a sturdy, bright-looking child, with straight corn-coloured hair and eyes exactly the same shade of arctic blue as her father's. She seemed curious, but not unfriendly, so Amelia smiled at her.

'I'm very pleased to meet you too. I have heard so much about you. Perhaps later on we can have a little chat and you can tell me more about my new home?' She turned to the other little girl, who was completely different from the older one. A tiny thing with dark curls and huge grey eyes in an elfin face, she looked both scared and wary at the same time.

Amelia smiled encouragingly at her to try and put her at ease, but she could see that it would probably take time to win her trust.

She decided to take things slowly so as not to frighten her.

Duty done, the girls ran to their father and gave him a hug and a kiss each. He managed to lift them both up at the same time and sat down on a sofa with them on his lap. The nanny, meanwhile, was still looking sour, and as soon as James had finished chatting to the girls, she whisked them out of the room saying it was time for their tea.

Amelia rose to go too, but James halted her with the words, 'Wait, what did you think of your new daughters?'

'I think they are delightful and I'm sure we shall deal very well together. Mathilde seems very confident and mature for her age and I think that if I give Chloe some time to get used to me, she will overcome her shyness.'

'Good,' he said in a softer tone than the one he had used earlier. 'I am aware that being a step-mother is not always easy and I shan't expect miracles, you know. I'll be happy if you just do your best.'

'Of course I will, I told you I like children.'

Amelia hesitated. 'There was one thing though...'

'Yes?'

'The nanny, has she been with them long? I mean, it's probably not my place to say so, but she looked a trifle severe to me.'

'I suppose you may be right, but nannies have to be a bit severe, don't they? I know mine always were. Discipline is necessary for children, don't you think? But you may do as you see fit – if you consider her unsuitable, by all means find someone else.'

'Thank you,' she said, feeling unaccountably happy that he trusted her judgement in this matter.

'Then everything is settled and I must be off if I am to get to Westfield before nightfall.'

'You are leaving so soon?'

'Yes, but don't worry, you will be well taken care of.'

Amelia was sure she would be, but not by the one person she really wanted to be with. She had hoped they could at least share a meal on her first night in her new home.

With a sigh she made her way back to her room, where she ordered an early dinner to be sent up on a tray. She couldn't face eating alone in the no doubt vast dining-room. It was easier to plead fatigue and eat in peace and quiet.

Amelia did not allow herself to feel lonely and bereft for long. Such foolishness did not have a place in an arranged marriage, she told herself, and she ought to be grateful to have this wonderful new home with everything she could possibly wish for and two lovely daughters into the bargain.

She was determined to make the best of everything and to prove to James that she could be an excellent wife and step-mother, then perhaps he would come back, she thought. The following morning she therefore dressed quickly in another of her new gowns, then sought out the housekeeper, who readily agreed to take her on a tour of the house. This occupied them until lunch-time and Amelia complimented Mrs Flint on her efficiency.

'You've left me nothing to do.' She smiled. 'Everything seems to be running smoothly.'

'Thank you, my lady, I'm glad you think so.' Mrs Flint looked pleased at the praise. 'I'll be sure to ask your opinion now that you're here. Will you be wanting to make any changes to the rooms?'

Although beautifully furnished in a rather old-fashioned style and spotlessly clean, Amelia felt some of the rooms needed a woman's touch. 'Well, I would like to change some of the curtains to lighter, less heavy and ornate materials, and perhaps add some cushions and the like to give this place a more homely feel. And there should be fresh flowers, if possible, don't you think?'

'An excellent idea, my lady. I'm sure the gardener will be only too happy to supply you with anything you need.'

'I'll seek him out after lunch then, I enjoy flower arranging. Could you be so kind as to find me plenty of vases, please?'

'Right away.'

Amelia had lunch in the morning-room,

acutely aware of the servants hovering behind her, no doubt wondering why her husband had abandoned her so soon, but she was still determined not to let it faze her. She was, however, happy to escape to the garden afterwards, having fetched a bonnet and shawl.

She walked along the well-kept paths in search of the head gardener. It was a lovely spring day, quite warm for May, and as the sun was strong she was glad her bonnet shaded her complexion from its glare. She finally tracked down the gardener in a remote corner of the rose garden.

'I'd be very happy to bring you flowers every day, my lady.' He beamed, when told what she wanted. 'I always thought it was a shame not to make use of some of these wonderful blooms.'

'You've done a marvellous job, this is such a lovely garden.' Amelia meant it and his smile widened even more at her praise.

Mission accomplished, Amelia retraced her steps slowly, enjoying the sunshine and the feeling that she was free from her aunt and the odious Bernard. Even if her situation here was not yet perfect, it was at least a great deal better than being her cousin's mistress.

Her thoughts were interrupted when she heard crying and shouting from behind a nearby hedge. She rushed around the corner, just in time to see Miss Downes slap little Chloe hard on the cheek, and shout at her, 'You naughty little thing, didn't I tell you to be careful of your new clothes? Now look what you've done, there's dirt all over your skirts.'

The nanny had Chloe's arm in a vice-like grip, and although Mathilde was trying to protect her sister by pulling on Miss Downes other arm, the woman shook her off easily.

Amelia saw red and stalked over to the little group, fury making her voice strong.

'How dare you hit your charges?' she shouted. 'Chloe is only four, for goodness' sake, a mere baby.' She almost snatched the child out of the surprised nanny's grip and lifted her into her arms to comfort her. She could feel Chloe quivering with fear and the little girl clung to Amelia as if her life depended on it, sobbing all the while.

'But look what she has done to her new clothes,' the nanny protested, white-faced now with both fear and anger. 'I can't have her behaving like a hoyden, she's forever getting dirty.'

Mathilde, who had by this time grasped the fact that they had an ally in Amelia, piped up. 'But she only fell down, Step-mama, and she didn't mean to, it was an accident.'

'Of course it was,' Amelia said soothingly, putting a hand on Mathilde's shoulder as well to reassure her. 'No four-year-old is going to fall down on purpose, that's a ridiculous notion. I suggest you moderate your discipline a little, Miss Downes, if you wish to retain your position in this household.'

The nanny glared at her. 'I'm not staying another minute,' she declared. 'You can look after them yourself, your ladyship.' The sneer in her voice as she emphasised Amelia's title was clear, as if the woman doubted she had a right to it. Amelia said nothing, however, and did not stop Miss Downes from stalking off towards the house.

'Good riddance,' she muttered.

'What does that mean?' Mathilde asked, looking puzzled.

Amelia smiled. 'It just means we're better off without her, don't you think?'

The little girl grinned. 'Oh, yes, she was hateful.'

Amelia decided to stay in the garden for a while, in order to give the nanny time to pack and leave before they returned to the house, and to this end she sat down on a nearby bench and cuddled Chloe, who was only hiccoughing slightly now. 'Come and sit by me, Mathilde, and tell me what you do all day. Do you have lessons or do you just play?'

'Nanny taught us things like how to behave, but we didn't have lessons, Step-mama. She said she was going to teach me to read and write maybe next year.'

'Hmm, if you ask me, you're old enough to learn already. Would you like me to teach you?'

'Yes please, Step-mama.'

The frequent use of that word was beginning to grate on Amelia as it didn't have a very nice ring to it.

'Do you think that perhaps you could call me Amelia instead? Step-mama sounds so … so hard,' she tried to find the right word for it. 'Perhaps later you can decide if you would like me to be your new mother, and then you can call me Mama if you wish, but until then we can just be friends and you call me by my name. How does that sound?'

Mathilde agreed readily, and even Chloe was heard to murmur, 'Melia.' 'I only called you that because Nanny said we had to,' Mathilde confided.

They walked slowly back to the house, chatting about the various flowers and birds in the garden, and held on to Amelia's hand all the way, as if it were a lifeline, and it was a touching gesture.

Back in the children's room, they were met by a frightened looking girl of about sixteen, who said her name was Eliza and that she was Miss Downes' helper in the nursery. Amelia asked Mathilde in a whisper whether she and Chloe liked Eliza, and when the child replied, 'Oh, yes, she's ever so nice to us,' Amelia came to a decision.

'Eliza, Miss Downes has left for good and from now on I would like you to assume the role of nanny to the children. I will see about finding them a governess soon, but for now you're in sole charge. Can you manage that?'

'Why yes, my lady, I'd be delighted to. I ... thank you, thank you so much.'

'And there will be no physical punishments, is that clear?'

'No, I would never hit them, I swear.'

'Good, that's all settled then. I shall come every morning to give the girls some lessons until I find a governess.'

She spent the rest of the afternoon in the nursery, taking tea with the children and playing with them and reading stories. They all had a very jolly time and she was almost sorry when it was time for her to go and change for dinner.

During the night, Amelia was awakened by a soft knock on her door. When she called 'Enter,' a very timid-looking Eliza came tiptoeing in, stammering excuses for having woken her ladyship.

'What's the matter?' Amelia sat up in bed and groped around on the table for a candle and matches.

'It's Miss Chloe, my lady, she had a nightmare and now she's crying and keeps asking for you. She says as how she won't go to sleep without you.'

Amelia put on a wrapper and followed the girl to the nursery. Chloe was indeed in a state and would only stop crying if Amelia stayed near. In the end, it seemed easier to simply carry the child to Amelia's bedroom and let her sleep with her. Mathilde, who didn't want to be left out, came too.

'It's just as well I have a huge bed,' Amelia muttered to herself, before sleep finally claimed them all, but deep inside she was pleased to have won the girls' trust. Somehow, she no longer felt so lonely.

CHAPTER EIGHT

The next day being Sunday, Amelia decided to attend the service at the local church with the girls, and to this end, after a leisurely breakfast taken in her bed amid much joking and giggling, she sent them off with Eliza to put on their Sunday best.

As she was unsure what kind of reception she would have from her new neighbours, after what James had told her about being ostracised by polite society, she took great care with her choice of outfit. She selected a prim walking dress of dark blue shot silk, with little white ruffs at the collar and cuffs and a matching Spencer and bonnet. It was elegant, but understated, and she thought it would do very well.

In the hall she encountered a worried-looking Mrs Flint, who asked whether her ladyship was really set on going to church.

Amelia smiled confidently. 'Don't worry, Mrs Flint. His lordship warned me things might be a trifle ... difficult, shall we say. It doesn't worry me in the least. Anyone has a right to worship in their local church, and so I shall tell them if they dare protest.'

'Oh, well if you're sure? I wish you luck, my lady.'

The little party arrived at the church in good time, and Amelia sailed up to the door regally, holding the girls by the hand. She was greeted by a very surprised and flustered vicar, who had no doubt recognised the grand carriage.

'Er, good morning, ma'am. I'm the Reverend Mr Denning.'

'And I am Lady Demarr and these are my step-daughters.' Amelia inclined her head to him, staring him straight in the eyes as if challenging him to deny her the right to enter.

'Ah, you're very welcome, my lady. If you will come this way, I'll show you to the family pew.'

This proved to be at the front of the church and Amelia swept past everyone, pretending to be unconcerned that they were all staring curiously at them. She sat down and waited for the service to begin.

James, in the meantime, was already regretting his self-imposed exile, and had nearly driven the grooms and workers at Westfield insane with his demands and counter-demands. His lordship was definitely not himself, they muttered to each other, something was eating the man. It was with a sigh of relief they greeted the news that he was going to ride over to Marr Place to see that all was well.

James had begun to feel guilty for leaving Amelia so abruptly and wanted to speak to her and try to make amends. Although he still felt that they should spend time apart, he realised now that he should perhaps have stayed a few days first to help ease her into her new role. He owed her an apology.

He arrived at his home early and was

greeted by Jamieson as usual.

'Where is Lady Demarr?' James demanded without preamble. 'I wish to see how she is going on.'

'I'm afraid she is not here, my lord.'

'Not here? What do you mean?' James was seized by a sudden fear. Had she left him already, angered by his behaviour towards her? The butler hastened to reassure him.

'She has merely gone to church, my lord.'

'To church?' James almost added, 'Is she mad?' but thought better of it. He was astonished that she would brave local society so soon after her arrival, then decided he had better go and help her face the tabbies. Even though he had warned her, he was genuinely concerned over the treatment she might receive from his uncharitable neighbours, who had snubbed him for the last few years.

He need not have worried though, as he soon found out. He entered the little church, only to stop dead in his tracks. There, in the front pew, was not merely his wife, but also his daughters. They all appeared totally unconcerned with everyone else in the church, and Amelia was singing the first hymn in her beautiful, clear voice, virtually on her own, aided only by the vicar's light tenor and Mathilde in her untrained fashion. Everyone else was staring at her with an open mouth, not uttering a sound.

With a smile, James walked up the aisle and sat down calmly next to Amelia, who looked up with surprise and almost faltered in her singing. He joined in the second verse with his strong baritone and after her initial astonishment, Amelia smiled at him almost conspiratorially. Together they sang the last verse as if no-one else existed.

When they had finished, there was complete silence for at least a full minute before Mr Denning cleared his throat and began the service.

Upon leaving the church, the vicar stopped them to thank them for coming. 'It is not often we have the benefit of such a lovely voice in our congregation,' he added to Amelia. 'I hope you will join us every Sunday from now on, your ladyship?'

'That is my intention, certainly,' Amelia replied.

The vicar introduced his wife, and after a slight nudge from her husband, Mrs Denning asked Amelia if she would care to come to tea at the vicarage one afternoon.

'I'd be delighted, thank you. Just send a note round to inform me which day would be suitable.' With a gracious smile, she swept back to the waiting carriage, again holding the little girls by the hand. She ignored everyone else, who stood in groups whispering and nodding in their direction. James handed them into the carriage, but when Mathilde begged to be allowed to ride on his horse, he let her sit in front of him in the saddle instead all the way home.

Amelia wondered what local society would make of that – the reviled Viscount showing himself to be a kind and caring father, as well as a supportive husband. No doubt there would be much speculation about this turn of events.

Amelia was uncomfortably aware of James's presence next to the carriage and whenever he looked in her direction, she felt overheated. She wondered who had brought him back so soon, but dared not ask.

'That was very brave of you, my dear,' he commented as he handed her down from the carriage. 'I think you were a success and if Mrs Denning invites you to tea, then the rest might follow. I congratulate you. I can see that there was no need for me to worry that you would come to regret our bargain.'

'Thank you, it was kind of you to come and lend me support. And of course I don't regret it, you told me what to expect and it is a great deal better to be a shunned Viscountess than an unpaid housekeeper.' He nodded, acknowledging the truth of that. 'Have you tired of life at Westfield already?' Amelia couldn't resist asking.

'No.' He frowned. 'If you must know I came to see how you were getting on and apologise for leaving you so abruptly the other day, but I see you are doing splendidly, so there was no need for me to come after all.'

'Well, I hope you will find time to join us again next week. It was much nicer to sing a duet with you than with the vicar.' On impulse, Amelia stood on tiptoe and kissed his cheek. 'Thank you, James,' she added, before turning to mount the stairs.

As she reached the top, she glanced over her shoulder and saw James standing trans-fixed, staring after her, with one hand hold-ing the cheek she had just kissed. Mathilde had to pull on his coat sleeve twice before he came out of his trance enough to say goodbye to the girls, and Amelia smiled to herself.

She rather thought she had given him something to think about.

The next few days were very busy. Amelia went to the nearest town to choose the materials for the new curtains and cushions she wanted to have made, and work began almost straight away. There was furniture to rearrange and the girls to teach, as well as such things as flower arranging and choosing the daily menus.

She also went to have tea with Mrs Denning, and impressed this lady to the extent that some of their other neighbours began to leave their cards at Marr Place.

Amelia decided to let them remain curious for a while and merely left her card in return instead of inviting them in, but there was one neighbour who was not content to be fobbed off in such a manner.

On the Friday morning, a booming female voice echoed round the hall. 'I demand to be taken to Lady Demarr at once. I am reliably informed that she has not gone out, so don't try to bamboozle me, my good man.'

Jamieson came to find Amelia, who was just taking tea in the morning room, and informed her that the local squire's wife and son would like to see her. Amelia, who had heard the loud exchange in the hall, smiled and asked him to show them into the small salon.

She tidied her hair quickly, then went to join her guests, a young man and a rather large matron. She noticed the young man first as he was wearing an embroidered waistcoat of a particularly loud shade of turquoise. This was teamed with an impossibly tight coat, high starched shirt points sticking out at the top and a cravat tied so intricately it must have taken him hours.

Amelia deduced that he was trying to ape the fashionable dandies, but with his sandy hair and youthful features, he merely looked like a young boy trying too hard to emulate his elders. Hiding a smile, Amelia turned to his mother instead.

'Lady Briggs, how nice of you to call.'

'Not at all, it was the least we could do after you regaled us with such fine singing last Sunday. This is Justin, my firstborn,' Lady Briggs announced grandly. 'Quite a nice boy, really, but a deplorable taste in waistcoats. Don't mind him.'

Young Mr Briggs did not look at all discomfited by his mother's remarks and Amelia guessed he must be used to it. He managed to bow over her hand with some grace, despite the tight coat, and as he smiled up at her she decided she rather liked him. He had a frank, open countenance and the look of admiration in his eyes, although blatant, was not in the slightest bit lecherous and she felt herself relax.

'Will you take some refreshment?' Amelia asked.

'A dish of tea would be very welcome, thank you. I am pleased to find that you are not at all high in the instep, my lady,' Lady Briggs confided, making Amelia smile inwardly again at her frankness. 'It's been many years since there was a Viscountess hereabouts, but I remember hearing that the last one was an insufferable snob.'

Amelia resolved to ask James about his mother at the earliest opportunity, but made no comment. She rang for tea, which soon arrived accompanied by scores of different cakes and some scones. It would seem that Cook was trying to impress her new mistress, as well as their guests, and young Mr Briggs in particular was very pleased with the offerings.

'I say, your cook must be a capital fellow,' he commented before tucking in with gusto.

'I believe "he" is actually a "she",' Amelia replied with a smile, 'but yes, she is indeed very good.'

Mr Briggs beamed at her and said over a mouthful of sponge cake, 'Do let mamma know if you ever wish to part with her.'

'Really, Justin, there is nothing wrong with our cook,' his mother protested, 'and we didn't come here to discuss food.' She turned to Amelia. 'I came to discuss parish business, your ladyship. Have you heard about the church fête next week?'

'No, I haven't. I take it this is a yearly event?'

'Yes, indeed. I am used to organising it, since my husband is the Squire, but now that you have taken up residence here, perhaps you would like to take over?' Lady Briggs looked as if this last sentence had had to be squeezed out of her and Amelia concluded that she didn't like her lofty position being usurped.

'Oh, no, Lady Briggs,' she said smoothly. 'I would be very happy if you could continue to run things. Everything here is very new to me, but perhaps you could be kind enough to assist me to learn, become my mentor as it were? I would deem it a great kindness.'

'Why of course, I would be only too pleased to offer you a few pointers.' Lady Briggs visibly preened herself. 'I'm sure you'll soon find your way around our little community.'

'I hope so. Tell me, do you think perhaps I ought to invite all the local ladies for tea one afternoon in order to become acquainted with everyone? If so, could I ask you to draw up a list of those I should invite?' Amelia felt sure that if Lady Briggs ordered them to come, then come they would.

'I say, why don't you have a regular dinner party?' put in Justin, who had by now managed to consume a considerable quantity of cake.

'Don't be a sapskull, my boy,' his mother told him roundly. 'I'm sure her ladyship needs some time to settle in before entertaining on a large scale. You're just trying to get yourself invited for dinner, aren't you?' Shaking her head, she added to Amelia, 'Honestly, I don't know where he puts it all.'

'Perhaps he leads a very active life?' She smiled at Justin again.

'Well, I ride a lot and hunt of course. I say, do you ride, Lady Demarr? Would you care to go for a ride with me one morning? I could show you the countryside hereabouts, there are some lovely views, you know.'

He looked so hopeful, Amelia didn't have the heart to disappoint him. 'Perhaps one morning,' she replied hesitantly, 'although I do have a lot to do at the moment.'

'Now don't go pestering her ladyship, Justin,' his mother cut in. 'Of course she doesn't have time to go junketing about with you.'

'It would only be for a short while,' he cajoled, looking at Amelia with puppy-like adoration.

'Very well,' Amelia capitulated. 'You may escort me on a short ride tomorrow morning, Mr Briggs. Would ten o'clock suit you?'

'Splendid!'

'I hope you don't regret your kindness, Lady Demarr,' his fond mother muttered darkly. 'But now we had better leave your ladyship in peace.' She rose and beckoned to her son with an imperious finger. 'Oh, there was one more thing, Lady Demarr. Would you mind very much honouring us with a small impromptu concert at the fête? A voice like yours should be heard singing more than hymns.'

'Well, I would have to ask my husband. I'm not sure he would approve.' Amelia was unwilling to risk putting James in a temper again. 'But I will see what he says.'

And with that Lady Briggs had to be satisfied.

Justin Briggs proved to be an amusing companion, full of youthful high spirits, and Amelia had an enjoyable ride with him. If she found his frequent adoring gazes a bit of a trial, she did not let on, but simply chatted about the scenery until his thoughts were diverted in another direction.

They found that they had many opinions in common, but although he was a year or two older than Amelia, she felt much more mature than him, perhaps because of all the trials she had been through. Nevertheless, they parted the best of friends, and now that she knew she had his support, and that of his mother, Amelia felt much better about going to church again the following day.

As she readied herself on the Sunday morning, Amelia had to suppress a slight flutter of excitement. She was looking for-ward to seeing James again, and although she told herself this was silly, she couldn't help it. It was obvious that he was not in a hurry to see her, since he had stayed away all week, but she still hoped to persuade him otherwise one day.

He was standing at the foot of the stairs, waiting to hand them all into the carriage. To Amelia's surprise, he jumped in after them, saying, 'I have decided to travel with you, it will present a better picture for the neighbours, don't you think?'

'Why yes, to be sure.' Amelia was more disturbed by his sudden nearness than she cared to admit and felt slightly breathless. As he was sitting next to her, with the girls facing them, their thighs brushed against each other as the carriage bumped along.

Amelia couldn't understand why his simply being close to her should have this strange effect, it was positively indecent the way she kept remembering how wonderful his kisses had been. How she wished he'd do it again...

Had she but known it, James's thoughts had been running along the same lines and he was feeling thoroughly frustrated. A week away from his wife had not given him the perspective he had craved, and he was no nearer to solving the problem of whether to trust her or not.

He wanted Amelia to be his wife in every sense, but he knew he must find a way of establishing her innocence once and for all first.

'Are you ready to face the dragons?' he asked, striving for some light conversation to relieve the tension.

'With you for protection, I can face anything, Sir Galahad,' she replied with a smile. James felt himself nearly drown in her violet blue gaze and turned away abruptly. This was not going at all well.

The church service was a penance as he struggled to keep his emotions under control. It was a relief when it was over, and he was pleasantly surprised when a few people actually came up to speak to them afterwards. He realised that Amelia had worked her magic on the neighbours as well and had broken the ice.

When Sir John and Lady Briggs greeted them loudly, he knew that his wife had achieved an absolute miracle in a very short space of time.

'Did dear Lady Demarr tell you about our little fête?' Lady Briggs demanded without preamble.

'I haven't had a chance to speak to my

husband about that yet,' Amelia put in quickly.

'Oh, but really, my lord, you must help me to persuade your wife to sing for us, I'm sure everyone would enjoy it immensely. Such a lovely voice. Do say you will add your persuasions to mine?' Lady Briggs was nothing if not determined when she was on a quest.

James, who could guess why Amelia had been reluctant to broach this subject with him, hastened to put her at ease. 'But of course she must sing for you if she wishes. I'm sure you'll be only too happy to oblige, won't you, my dear?'

He looked at Amelia and smiled so that she would understand that it was his way of atoning for his actions in London. She nodded almost imperceptibly.

'I can only give in with good grace, Lady Briggs. Let us discuss it in more detail at my tea party.'

James stared at Amelia in surprise, but refrained from asking any questions until they were back in the carriage.

'Tea party?' he enquired with raised eye-brows.

'Oh, it is nothing really. I've invited a few of the local ladies in order to become better acquainted with them. Lady Briggs was kind enough to give me a list of names.'

James nodded appreciatively. 'That was very clever of you, my dear. With Lady Briggs on your side, you'll soon win everyone over.'

'That was my intention.' Amelia smiled. 'Would you care to come?'

'Me? Good lord, no! A room full of women taking tea and chattering like hens is not my idea of fun. I will leave that to you.'

James turned to his daughters and began to chat to them instead. He felt altogether too happy with his wife's achievements and decided he was at risk of forgetting his mis-givings if he talked to her for much longer.

'Tell me what you two have been up to this week,' he invited.

'We're doing lessons with Amelia,' Mat-hilde informed him, looking very proud. 'I can read some words already and Amelia says I'm a fast learner.'

'Me, too,' put in Chloe, not wanting to be outdone. 'C-A-T,' she pronounced the letters in an exaggerated fashion.

James smiled. 'I'm glad you're all getting along. What's this about lessons?' He looked to Amelia for an answer.

'I decided it was time the girls learned their alphabet and such things, and with Miss Downes no longer there, I thought it best if I gave them lessons myself.'

'Miss Downes is gone?' James remembered Amelia's comments about the nanny and wondered if he had given Amelia too much power since she had seemingly dismissed the nanny straight away. Chloe's next words made him think again.

'She hit me,' the little girl told her father, her eyes big and grave in her tiny face. 'Lots of times. And shouted at me.'

'Yes, and all because Chloe fell down. It wasn't even her fault,' Mathilde added.

'I see. Well in that case, I'm glad she is gone. So who looks after you now?'

'Eliza and Melia,' Chloe said.

'Eliza was the nanny's helper,' Amelia explained hurriedly. 'The girls told me she was kind to them, so I thought in the circumstances...'

'That sounds like an excellent solution.' James only vaguely remembered employing a young girl, but if Amelia thought her suitable, then no doubt she was. 'But will you want to continue teaching the girls?'

'Well, I was thinking that they probably need a proper governess, and as it happens, I have just heard that my old governess, Miss Keys, is available. Would you consider her for the position? She was very kind to me, but firm.'

'She sounds ideal. By all means, write to her.'

'Thank you.'

James could see that Amelia had everything in hand, but he could not shake the thought that she was too good to be true. It was a relief when he could finally take his leave and go back to Westfield, where he could think clearly again without Amelia's nearness disturbing his senses.

He simply had to find a solution to his problem, or he would go mad.

CHAPTER NINE

James had his worst fears confirmed only two days later. Riding through the woods of his estate, he spotted a pair of riders in the distance at the top of a ridge. As he rode closer, he realised that one of them was Amelia and she was leaning over to whisper something in the ear of her rather handsome escort, a young man with sandy-coloured hair and a blindingly green jacket. The pair appeared to be alone, with no grooms in attendance for the sake of propriety.

James saw red.

Spurring his horse into a gallop, he soon reached the laughing pair, and skidded to a halt next to them.

'I say, watch out, sir, or you'll have us all over the precipice,' the young man protested, his horse having taken exception to James's abrupt arrival. James ignored him and scowled at Amelia.

'Hello, James,' she said, looking at him with a slight frown. 'Is something amiss? It's not the girls, is it?'

'Perhaps if you were at home, instead of gallivanting around with your beau, you would know the answer to that yourself,' James replied, his voice hard. He saw Amelia flinch, a look of hurt entering her eyes.

'They were perfectly fine when I left for my short ride with Justin,' she said. 'They were playing games with Eliza.'

'Justin, is it?' James turned to the young man and fixed him with a glare. He had no idea who he was, but vaguely recalled seeing him at church the previous Sunday. The man bowed in the saddle.

'Justin Briggs, at your service, my lord.'

'And my wife's, it would seem,' James murmured. He did not bow back, but turned pointedly to Amelia instead. 'I was coming over to see how you were getting on, but I see you're doing just fine, so I'll take my leave. Good day to you.'

He turned and galloped off in a flurry of hooves, and it was only later, when he had calmed down slightly, that he realised he had almost run down one of his own grooms on the way. A groom who was obviously there to chaperone his wife.

She hadn't been alone with young Briggs after all.

Amelia had decided that the girls may as well eat their meals with her when they had no guests, to save the servants the trouble of taking food up to the nursery. She thought it would be good for them to learn some table manners as well.

Consequently, the three of them had just sat down to lunch when there was a great commotion in the hall. Amelia ignored it at first, but the voices became louder, and eventually she went to see what was happening.

A frail looking elderly gentleman stood in the middle of the hall, arguing with his valet and with Jamieson. His face was rapidly turning puce as he became more and more agitated, and Amelia thought it best to intervene.

'Can I be of assistance, sir?' she asked. 'I'm Lady Demarr. His lordship is not at home at the moment.'

The old man looked her over, then seemingly decided that he liked what he saw, smiled and said, 'Yes, my dear, you can most certainly be of assistance. Tell these two fools to go about their business and leave me alone. I'm not yet in my dotage, I don't need coddling at every turn and I most definitely do not wish to lie down for a nap, having come all this way to see my grandson's new wife.'

'Oh, you must be the Earl of Holt then. Welcome to Marr Place, my lord. I'm afraid that no-one informed me you were coming, or I would have had everything ready for you.' Amelia curtseyed to him, but he reached out for her hands and kissed each one in turn in a rather old-fashioned way, which she found charming.

'Don't worry your pretty little head about that,' said Lord Holt. 'If these two would just get on with their duties, I'm sure they'll have a room ready for me in a trice. I decided to visit on the spur of the moment, since I felt quite well this morning. With the gout, I never know how matters will stand from one day to the next, you see.'

He took a deep breath. 'And since my scamp of a grandson hasn't seen fit to bring his bride to me, I had perforce to come and see for myself. An old man can't wait forever.'

Amelia couldn't resist a smile at this and, ignoring the pleading glances from Jamieson and the valet, she invited his lordship into the morning room to partake of lunch.

'Excellent idea,' he said. 'And who have we here then?'

Mathilde was staring at him curiously, while Chloe jumped off her chair to run and hide behind Amelia's skirts.

'These are your great-granddaughters, my lord, Mathilde and Chloe. Make your curtseys to Lord Holt, girls, please.' This they did, but continued to stare in fascination at the old man.

'Oh, sit down, do,' he waved a hand at them. 'I shan't eat you, you know. I'm much too old for that. And anyway, I don't have enough teeth left.' Mathilde giggled and Chloe's eyes grew round as saucers. 'I'm glad to have met you at last. I have been ill for a long time, or I would have come to see you before.' He winked at the girls and they began to relax.

He allowed Amelia to serve him with 'a few choice morsels' as he put it, which, had he seen it, would have given his doctor a fit, consisting as they did of all the things he had expressly forbidden his lordship to eat. Amelia suspected this might be the case, but was tactful enough not to argue.

The old man seemed more interested in talking anyway, and didn't actually eat very much. He regaled them with tales of all the pranks Lord Demarr had got up to as a boy and soon had them all chuckling, even Chloe.

'And now I had better retire for a rest,' he said at last, 'else I'll have no respite from the nagging of my servants. Perhaps you could all join me in my room for an early dinner and we can chat some more?'

'Oh, yes please, great-grandfather,' the girls chorused. Amelia agreed.

The evening meal was even merrier and his lordship's valet was shaking his head at such goings-on, but it seemed to be doing Lord Holt a deal of good. When the girls were led off to bed by Eliza, he asked Amelia to stay on for a game of chess, and she willingly obliged.

'I have to warn you, though, I am not a very good player, as my father was wont to tell me.'

'As to that, we shall see, but tell me about your father. He was Colonel Ravenscroft, I understand. I knew him a little, and have heard many good things about him.'

'Many bad ones too, no doubt.' Amelia made a small face. 'Although he adored his life in the Army and was very conscientious in his duties and well liked, illness forced him to retire prematurely and then I'm afraid he succumbed to the lure of the gaming tables a little too often. He ... shot himself just over a year ago now.'

After a slight hesitation, Amelia told Lord Holt the rest of her story and how she had met his grandson, leaving nothing out, not even the misunderstanding at the opera. The old man was so perspicacious, she thought he would find out anyway and as she liked him a lot already, she wanted to be truthful with him.

'And where is James now?' Lord Holt asked when she had finished.

'He's at Westfield. He said we needed time apart to get used to our marriage. To be honest, I think he is regretting it already, but it is done now and to my mind, we have to make the best of it.'

Lord Holt nodded. 'Indeed, and you seem

to have made a good start. Don't think I didn't notice the changes in this house – all for the better – and those little girls have obviously taken to you.'

'Oh, I haven't achieved much yet, but I do wish he'd come back.'

'Don't worry, he will and he'll soon see that he's made an excellent choice of wife.'

'You're too kind.'

'Not at all. I am neither stupid nor blind yet and I'm very glad James found you. Just give him some time, he's always been a stubborn boy, but he'll see sense in the end, don't you fret.'

They parted on very good terms and Amelia thought wistfully that she seemed to get on well with all of James's family. The only one she couldn't please was him. It was a lowering thought, but Lord Holt seemed to think there was still hope, and that bolstered her courage.

Somehow, she would make this marriage a success.

James felt like a fool for jumping to conclusions. For two days he had stayed away, knowing he owed Amelia an apology yet again, but unable to decide how best to approach the subject. If he told her that he had acted out of jealousy, which he now realised was the case, it would be tantamount to admitting that he wanted their marriage to be much more than one of convenience.

However, he still felt it was too early in their relationship for him to trust her fully, and for him to admit such a thing would give her the upper hand.

What he really needed to know, was whether she was indeed pregnant or not. As yet, he had seen no sign of this, but he knew that on some women it need not be visible for quite some time. He was loath to ask her outright, but neither could he find out in any other way. Besides, she had already denied it.

He finally decided to tackle the problem head on and to that end, he took himself off to Marr Place once again. Upon his arrival, however, the house seemed deserted and he had to search for quite a while before he found even a footman.

'Everyone's outside, m-my lord,' the youth stammered. 'On the terrace.'

James headed for the back of the house and stepped out through the French doors, then stopped dead at the unexpected sight of his wife and daughters having lunch with his grandfather.

To James's further amazement, Lord Holt was sitting with little Chloe on his lap, telling a very amusing story, judging by the gales of laughter coming from all his listeners, and the whole scene was one of contentment and togetherness. James was annoyed to find that he felt left out.

'Grandfather, it's been a long time since we had the pleasure of your company here,' he said, somewhat stiffly as he went over to make his bow.

'James, my boy, there you are. I had to come over and entertain your family since you were off gallivanting about goodness knows where.'

'I am very pleased that you were able to make the journey. Had I known, I would have invited you sooner. I trust you are not too fatigued? Should you not be resting?'

'Bah! Go and join those other two killjoys in there,' Lord Holt waved a hand vaguely towards the house. 'They don't want a body to enjoy himself, now do they, my sweet?'

He addressed this last to Chloe, who giggled and said, 'No, they bully you awfully, don't they.'

James blinked in surprise as Lord Holt laughed and said, 'You see, out of the mouths of babes...'

James had to smile; the entire scenario was too fantastic for him to take it in. When pressed, he consented to take lunch with them all, protesting vigorously when his grandfather embarked on yet another tale about his youthful misdemeanours.

He joined in the laughter, however, and glanced at Amelia from time to time. She looked happy and content and the sight of her like that made him feel warm all over.

He wanted her to look like that always.

'You look very charming today,' he commented. She was wearing a pretty morning dress of lilac sprigged muslin, which matched her eyes and complemented her hair. She gave no sign that she was annoyed with him for his rudeness to young Mr Briggs and this gave him hope that they may come to some understanding.

'Thank you.' A slight blush stained her cheeks, but she seemed pleased with the compliment.

The afternoon passed and James decided to stay at Marr Place for the night so that he could spend more time with his grandfather. He thought it best to put off his chat with Amelia until the next day, as he didn't want to spoil the mood.

'Could you spare me a moment, please? I'd like a word with you in the library.'

Amelia looked up from the flower arrangement she had been finishing off and nodded at her husband. 'Of course.' She followed him across the beautiful hall, so light and airy in the spring sunshine, wondering what he wished to talk to her about.

'Please, sit down. This won't take long.'

Amelia waited while he collected his thoughts, pacing back and forth in front of her.

'Amelia, as you are aware, I'm heir to an earldom. This carries with it certain duties and responsibilities, including that of begetting an heir myself.' Amelia felt her cheeks grow hot, but she remained silent.

'At the time of our marriage, I despaired of finding anyone at such short notice and your offer came as a welcome surprise.

'However, I only checked your background briefly with those present at the ball and I have come to think that perhaps I acted rashly. I should have taken more time to satisfy myself as to your suitability.'

Amelia frowned. 'Are you saying I'm not good enough to be your wife?'

'No. Yes. I mean, I don't know – that's the whole point. I know nothing about you really. The thing is, as and when you present me with an heir, I have to be sure that he is actually mine.'

'You are accusing me of unfaithfulness already?' Amelia stood up, her fists clenched, ready for battle. She could not believe what she was hearing.

'Not exactly. What I'm saying is that you could already be carrying a child, intending to pass it off as mine.' Amelia gasped, but he ignored her and continued with what sounded like a rehearsed speech. 'I must make sure this is not the case, therefore I have invited an eminent physician from Harley Street, Dr Augustus Harcourt, who is a specialist in obstetrics. He should be arriving later this afternoon and I would be very grateful if you would allow him to examine you.' He stopped directly in front of her, fixing her with his gaze.

'Of all the low-down... No! I most certainly do not want to be examined by some stranger I've never met.'

'Amelia, please,' he pleaded quietly. 'I

need to know that I haven't been duped. I want to trust you, really I do, but a part of me tells me that I've acted like a fool and…'

'You most certainly have.' Amelia was so angry; she hardly knew what to do with herself. 'And to think I was beginning to like you. Hah! Very well, I will allow the good doctor to paw me, but you can forget your heir in any case for I don't ever wish to speak to you again.'

With her head held high, she turned and marched out of the room.

Dr Harcourt proved to be a very nice, rotund little man and the examination consisted merely of him prodding her abdomen from the outside.

'You couldn't possibly be carrying even a two-month old baby,' he declared. 'There is nothing there at all.' When Amelia did not reply, he very wisely said no more, simply bowed courteously and took his leave, presumably to report his findings to Lord Demarr.

During the days that followed, Amelia made it perfectly clear to her husband that she wanted nothing to do with him. She treated him coldly, hardly speaking to him at all unless asked a direct question. To her amazement, everyone in the house appeared to be siding with her and she guessed that somehow they had all got wind of what had happened.

She supposed it was inevitable that everyone in a house like this would know everything going on, but it was still disconcerting. The servants tiptoed about, giving James strange looks, and Jamieson even went so far as to drop a glass of wine in James's lap. Although he apologised profusely, it was clear to Amelia that it had been done on purpose.

Lord Holt kept shaking his head every time he looked at his grandson and even the girls did not go out of their way to talk to their father. They had understood that Amelia was angry with him for some reason, and they wanted her to be happy again.

In the end, James took himself off to Westfield once more, muttering about 'not being wanted in his own home.' Amelia breathed a sigh of relief.

Two days later, Miss Keyes, her former governess, arrived at last to take up her new position. Amelia was delighted to see her, as they had been very close, and took her up to her room without delay.

'Well now, haven't you landed on your feet, young lady,' Miss Keyes commented with a smile as she looked around her. 'I never thought you'd end up a Viscountess, not in my wildest dreams.'

'Neither did I, but much good it has done me.' Amelia proceeded to tell her old friend and mentor everything that had happened, ending with the recent visit of the doctor, but to her surprise Miss Keyes did not take her side, as everyone else had.

'Your husband sounds like a very sensible man to me,' she said.

'Sensible? Surely you don't mean that you think him right in believing the worst of me?' Amelia demanded indignantly.

'No, of course not, but one cannot but see why he felt he had to do what he did.' Miss Keyes put her hand on Amelia's arm in a soothing gesture. 'You really did not know each other very well, did you, and perhaps he has been hurt by a woman before. Did you not mention something about a scandal?'

'Well, yes, but...'

'Do you know any of the facts about it?' Amelia shook her head, beginning to see her friend's point. 'Precisely. And with Sir Bernard going round telling all and sundry that you were his mistress, he did have cause to doubt you. Often there is no smoke without a fire, as they say.'

'But he shouldn't have married me if he believed that,' Amelia protested.

'Perhaps not, but you both acted rashly, did you not? You married him without knowing what scandal he had caused. I think you should give the poor man a chance to make it up to you. I'm sure everything will work out in the end.'

'I don't know. I'll think about it. Anyway, it's lovely to have you here and I hope the girls will like you as much as I do.'

'Well, let's go and meet them and find out.'

CHAPTER TEN

When the doctor told him the verdict, James was aware of a feeling of great relief, but also shame that he had not trusted his wife. She had never appeared to be the sort of woman who dissimulated, unlike his first wife, and he wished now that he had listened to his intuition where Amelia was concerned.

But now it was too late.

Sitting all alone at Westfield, night after night, he at first tried to drown his problems with brandy, but upon waking up for the third day in a row with a mammoth headache, he knew that was not the solution.

There had to be some way of earning Amelia's forgiveness, and the only way he would find out was to go back to Marr Place.

He decided to ask his grandfather for advice. Amelia seemed to like the old man and James knew that Lord Holt was a wise old bird who missed nothing. If anyone knew what to do, it would be him.

Before he had time to do so, however, Amelia surprised him by demanding to speak to him the minute he walked through the door. It was as if she had been lying in wait to pounce on him the moment he returned.

'Yes, of course. In the library?'

Amelia nodded. As soon as they were inside, with the door firmly closed, she turned to him, looking nervous, but determined. 'We really cannot go on like this,' she said. 'The discord between us is affecting the children, and much as I appreciate their support, I feel it is wrong that they should take sides against their own father.'

'What exactly are you proposing that we do about it?' he asked carefully.

'Well, I thought perhaps we could declare a truce and at least pretend to be friends again. After all, that was our original bargain, was it not? We could try to put what happened behind us.'

'Could you do that? Amelia, I swear I will never doubt you again. I am profoundly sorry for any hurt I caused you. I really wasn't just thinking of myself, you know, but my family's honour.' He smiled ruefully. 'I'm sure Grandfather would say that was the first time I've done so, but I have never intentionally set out to damage my good name.'

Amelia held out her hand. 'A truce then?'

'A truce,' he agreed, clasping her hand with both his and wishing that he could take her into his arms instead. That would have to wait though, as he felt he had to somehow earn her trust again. 'Perhaps we should take the children for a picnic this afternoon? It looks like a beautiful day and we can show them that we are friends again.'

'That's a good idea. I'll go and speak to Cook immediately.'

Summer began in earnest and they had a few weeks of perfect sunshine, blue skies and only a slight breeze to stir things up a bit. After that first outing, they decided to take advantage of the weather and organised such trips almost every other day, sometimes alone with the children, sometimes accompanied by Lord Holt and Miss Keyes.

There were plenty of things to see in the neighbouring countryside, beautiful vistas and shady forest glades, and they set out for these jaunts with picnic hampers filled to the brim by the cook.

The children relaxed again and blossomed in this new peaceful environment, and even began to call Amelia 'Mama' instead of her name. This pleased her greatly, of course, and James seemed happy with this as well.

'I am glad Chloe is not so timid any more,' he commented one afternoon as they were lying side by side in the shade of a huge oak tree, watching the girls play with a ball nearby.

'Yes, she seems to have come out of her shell at last. It's strange how different they are both in looks and temperament, though,' Amelia added.

'It's not really that strange,' James said slowly. 'They are only half-sisters after all.'

'What do you mean? Were you married twice before?'

'No, but I'm afraid that my former wife was not entirely faithful to me. In fact, after she produced Mathilde, we never again shared a bed, so I know for a fact that Chloe is not mine.'

Amelia was speechless for a moment before finding her tongue again. 'And yet you acknowledged her as yours? That was very kind of you.'

'Not really. Since she is a girl, she doesn't affect the succession of the earldom after all, and I simply could not bear to have her adopted or given to someone who may not care for her. I felt her place was with her sister and I have come to love her as much as I do my own child.'

Amelia was amazed by his revelation. She had come to realise that he had a generous nature, but to take in another man's child without ever differentiating between the children was truly noble in her eyes.

'I love them both equally as well,' she said.

'I'm glad. You make a wonderful mother.'

He was looking at her as if he wanted to make her a mother for real and Amelia found herself wishing that he would, but at the last moment he pulled back and didn't so much as kiss her.

Amelia sighed inwardly. These last few weeks had shown her that Miss Keyes had been right, but now she didn't know how to let James know that she had forgiven him. She wanted to start afresh, but how to tell him?

James was waging a daily battle against himself as the urge to make Amelia his in every way was getting stronger all the time. He was determined to be patient and give her time to forgive him for not trusting her, but he was becoming more and more frustrated. He thought he detected signs of her softening towards him, but he couldn't be sure. Perhaps he should simply ask?

As he paced his library one afternoon, wondering how best to phrase his question, a visitor was announced. It was a rather dishevelled and travel-stained Bootle, Lady Marsh's erstwhile butler.

'This is a surprise. What brings you here?' James asked, greeting the man with pleasure. 'Have you finally left the old dragon's employ and come for those references we promised you?'

'Not exactly, my lord.' Bootle looked grave. 'I'm afraid I've come to warn you. Sir Bernard has somehow got wind of your marriage – some army fellow he met in London let slip that he had seen you with your new bride and congratulated him on the exalted connection. He was in a rare taking, I can tell you.

'Ranting and raving about Miss Amelia's duplicity, low morals and I don't know what else besides. He has sworn to pay her back somehow, and even his mother's strictures failed to calm him down. I'm right fearful for Miss Amelia's safety.'

'I see. Well thank you for coming to warn us. You must of course remain here until you can find another position. I'm sure you could do with a rest after coming all this way.'

'Perhaps I could help you keep an eye on Miss Amelia?'

'That's a good idea. It would be best if we didn't worry her with this news though. I'll just take precautions so that no-one can slip in unnoticed and tell the staff to be vigilant.'

That same afternoon saw the arrival of yet another surprise visitor, this one initially not as welcome. He demanded to see Lady Demarr immediately.

'I regret her ladyship is not at home, sir,' Jamieson informed him.

'Well, what about his lordship then? Damn it man, it's a very serious matter!'

'I shall inform his lordship of your presence. If you would care to wait in here?' He showed the guest into the front parlour and went in search of his master.

'Captain Marshall, what brings you here?' James was not at all pleased to see the man who had seemed so friendly with Amelia.

'My apologies for intruding in this fashion, my lord, but I have news of a possible threat to your wife.' Captain Marshall grabbed James's arm in some agitation and shook it slightly. 'I was greatly disturbed by an occurrence reported to me by a fellow officer yesterday.'

'And what might that have been?' James disentangled himself unobtrusively.

'The man is a gaming companion of someone named Sir Bernard Marsh, who claims to be Lady Demarr's cousin, only he called her by her maiden name and told the fellow he'd been searching high and low for her. He seemed distraught and the officer, who had been told the good news about Miss Amelia's marriage, thought to put Sir Bernard at ease by telling him.

'Only, it had the strangest effect – the man went berserk, screaming about revenge. When the officer tried to remonstrate with him, he actually knocked him down. I thought I had better come straight here to warn you.'

'Thank you, Captain, that was very kind of you. I appreciate your concern for my wife. You needn't worry though, I had already been warned by Sir Bernard's butler, and I'm taking every precaution in order to protect her.'

'Well, thank goodness for that!'

'Yes, and I'm rather glad you didn't catch my wife at home, because I think it best not to worry her with this. It's better if we keep it to ourselves, don't you think?'

'Oh yes, females having delicate sensibilities and all that. Of course. I quite understand.'

'Now, I'll have Jamieson show you up to a guest room. I trust you'll stay overnight at least? You can always tell my wife that you wanted to come and see for yourself that she

153

was all right.'

'Splendid idea, thank you. Delighted to stay for a short visit and you can count on me,' he tapped his nose with his index finger, 'mum's the word.'

Although not a bluestocking in the true sense of the word, Amelia had read widely and her father had delighted in teaching her subjects that were normally only taught to boys.

Consequently, she knew her understanding to be superior, and it irked her to be treated like an imbecile. This was precisely the feeling that she had that afternoon.

First, there was Bootle, telling her some cock-and-bull story about how he couldn't stand Lady Marsh and her mean ways another moment and had decided to come and ask Lord Demarr for the promised reference. This was of course reasonable enough, apart from the fact that Lady Marsh's mean ways had never affected him before.

Next, there was Captain Marshall, with yet another strange tale of how he and his fellow officers had been worrying about her sudden marriage and had decided he had better visit her to make sure everything was as it should be.

Amelia couldn't understand why they should suddenly start to worry about her after so many weeks, when it was surely too late to do anything about it anyway. Besides, she had already told him that she was fine when they met in London.

When she found her husband having a whispered conversation with an individual of dubious appearance in the hallway, however, she decided that enough was enough.

'May I have a word with you please, James.' Amelia crossed her arms over her chest and fixed him with a glare.

'But of course, my dear, any time.' The strange individual cast her a furtive glance, then sidled off. 'What can I do for you?'

'Who was that man?'

'Oh, just one of the estate workers.'

'Then why were you whispering?'

'Were we? I don't recall us doing so, we

were merely discussing a small matter of a boundary.'

Amelia was not convinced. 'I see. I don't suppose you know the real reasons for Bootle's or Captain Marshall's arrivals here today, do you? I don't believe a word of those Canterbury tales they told me.'

'Real reasons? Why, whatever can you mean?' James's guileless look didn't fool Amelia for a moment.

'Very well, have it your way. There is something fishy going on, but if you won't tell me, I shall just have to get it out of Bootle. And to think I thought we were finally beginning to trust each other. You may consider our truce at an end until you are prepared to treat me as an intelligent human being.'

'But Amelia...'

She stalked off without listening to any of his protests. She knew they would be lies anyway and this put her in a foul mood. What she needed was a good gallop, she decided, to work off her frustrations and with that in mind, she went straight upstairs and changed into her riding habit. It was not long before she was out on her favourite mare, cantering down the drive all by herself.

'But my lady, shouldn't I come with you?' the head groom had asked anxiously.

'There is no need, Hanning. I intend to ride only on Demarr property.' Amelia wanted to be alone and having a groom tag along would only slow her down. The groom tried to protest further, but she cut him short and set off.

She rode the horse hard for half an hour, letting the animal have her head for a good gallop on even ground, and she finally began to feel slightly calmer. The exercise soothed her and she tried to think rationally about her husband's behaviour.

He had definitely been hiding something, but perhaps she had been hasty in thinking that it must be something bad. What if he was organising a surprise for her? This thought made her feel guilty, but she shrugged it off. She would just have to wait and see.

Trotting through a small copse, she suddenly heard the sound of hoof beats behind her and a feeling of foreboding came over her, so strong that on impulse she urged her horse into a gallop once more. She tried to look over her shoulder, but could see nothing, until suddenly a rider came hurtling out of the forest to her right. Amelia's horse swerved, but she managed to stay in the saddle and was relieved to see that the horseman was only Justin Briggs. They reined in their mounts.

'Lady Demarr, are you all right? I thought your horse had bolted, so I was trying to rescue you.'

'No, no, I was fine. It was just … I thought I was being followed by someone and I'm afraid I panicked.'

'That's understandable.' Justin peered behind them with a frown. 'Would you like me to go and investigate?'

'No, thank you. If there was anyone there, I'm sure he is probably long gone now that you are here. I would very much appreciate your escort home though, if you wouldn't mind.'

'I'd be only too delighted to be of assistance.'

'You won't tell anyone about this, will you? I don't want people to think me foolish and fanciful.'

'Of course not. You have my word.'

Amelia spent a restless night, tossing and turning. Whenever she fell asleep, she had vivid dreams of being chased through a forest by an unseen nemesis and woke up with her heart beating a frantic tattoo.

In the end, she decided to go for a walk round the gardens just after dawn. She would not get any more sleep this night and the fresh air would calm her nerves.

She slipped out the back door and stood for a moment savouring the birdsong and the wonderful smell of newly-mown grass. As she began to walk along the well-kept paths, she felt soothed by the beauty all around her.

Her steps took her farther and farther

away from the house, but she didn't notice. She was deep in thought, wondering what to do about the situation between James and herself.

She wanted him to be her husband in every way.

No matter what he had done, no matter how infuriating he could be, she knew now that she loved him. Until this latest set-back, they had been getting on famously, and there had been several occasions when she had thought he might kiss her, but for some reason he had held back even though she was sure she had seen desire in his eyes. Was he still unsure? Or was he just waiting for her to make the first move?

With the early morning sunshine lifting her spirits, Amelia's positive nature came to the fore and she decided that if she wanted her marriage to be real, she had to take the first step. If James rejected her, then so be it, but nothing ventured, nothing gained. She would ask to speak to him in private, then she would kiss him and see what his reaction was.

It was a bold plan, but if it worked, it would be worth it.

Before she could return to the house to ready herself for the day ahead, a pair of strong arms came out of nowhere to encircle her from behind and a cold voice said, 'Well, well, it must be my lucky day.'

CHAPTER ELEVEN

Amelia froze. She recognised that hateful voice only too well, the voice that had tormented her for months and which she had hoped never to hear again.

'Cousin Bernard, to what do I owe this dubious pleasure?' She tried to sound braver than she felt and hoped that he didn't hear the slight catch in her voice. She tried to free herself from his grip, but he was much stronger than her, so her struggles were to no avail. A cold feeling of dread settled in the pit of her stomach.

'Now, now, my dear, haven't I told you again and again that you really must strive to be nice to me?' he chided, a note of triumph in his voice, as he knew he had the upper hand at last. 'That was a nasty little trick you played on me, running away like that. But now I've found you again and this time, you won't be going anywhere.'

'Release me! My husband will be here any moment,' Amelia hissed, continuing to struggle in vain.

'I don't think so. I've been reconnoitring and the last time I looked, he was fast asleep.'

'You were inside the house?'

'No, he's in a chair in the library, I saw him from the window. Too much brandy last night, I should think. You won't be seeing him for a while.' Bernard chuckled and the sound sent another frisson of fear snaking through Amelia.

She opened her mouth to scream for help,

but Bernard anticipated this and clamped his hand over her mouth.

'Don't make me hurt you already, I want to take my time.' Amelia made the mistake of glancing over her shoulder at him and saw him grinning as if the thought of hurting her gave him infinite pleasure. 'Besides, I don't think your husband will miss you. I heard rumours in the village that your marriage isn't working out quite the way you had hoped.'

'That's not true. James loves me,' Amelia said, hoping against hope that this was true. Even if it was, however, it wouldn't help her now. In a last ditch attempt to free herself, she kicked Bernard on the shin, but her thin slippers did hardly any damage at all and he merely laughed.

'Oh, I do like spirited women, cousin. It will be a pleasure to tame you, but not here. Come on, let's go.'

James woke up with a crick in his neck and realised that he had fallen asleep in the library the previous evening. He had been having a drink while he pondered whether he ought to tell Amelia about Bernard or not, and he must have nodded off.

She had been right, he knew that now. As she was a sensible female and not the kind who had the vapours for every little thing, he was sure she would have coped with the knowledge that her cousin wanted revenge on her. It would also have put her on her guard so that she didn't go haring off riding without anyone to accompany her. James had never felt so relieved in his life as when he was told she had come back unscathed.

He loved her.

There was no doubt in his mind any longer. Amelia was the woman he wanted to spend the rest of his life with, to protect and cherish. He couldn't bear the thought of anything happening to her. In fact, he was going to go and tell her this minute, even though it was barely morning.

Taking the stairs two at a time, he reached her room in record time and opened the door slowly so as not to wake her too abruptly. He tiptoed over to the big bed, but to his surprise it contained only his two daughters. Mathilde heard him step on a creaking floorboard and raised her head.

'Papa?'

'Shh, sweetheart, I just came to talk to Mama. Do you know where she is?'

'She said she was going to the garden.'

'Garden? Oh, no…' Mathilde frowned, so he hurried to reassure her. 'You go back to sleep, while I go and find her.'

Icy tentacles gripped his insides as he raced down the stairs. He found the French windows to the morning room unlocked and rushed outside, following the paths towards the rose garden.

Once out of earshot of the house, he began to call Amelia's name, but there was no reply. Eventually he realised that he needed help and ran back to the house to organise a search party.

Amelia wondered if she had ever been so uncomfortable or so afraid in her life. Lying on top of some rotten straw in an old barn,

165

she knew not where, with her arms tied behind her, she was waiting for Bernard to come back.

'I'm going to procure us a conveyance as my horse can't carry us both,' he had informed her. 'I want to be as far away as possible from this place before nightfall, and then we can enjoy the evening together.'

Amelia shivered. Bernard's handkerchief was stuffed into her mouth and tied tight with a scarf, so there was no chance of calling for help. She felt as if she couldn't breathe properly, but tried not to panic.

Her hands were bound securely with a thin rope, and although she tried to work the knots loose, they wouldn't budge so much as an inch.

What would become of her if Bernard succeeded in his evil scheme, she wondered? She very much doubted her husband would want her back and she couldn't blame him. He might revenge himself on Bernard, but it would be too late for Amelia. Then he would surely divorce her. That thought was too awful to contemplate.

Frustration boiled up inside her, quelling the fear for a while, but it soon returned when she heard the sound of horses' hooves. Bernard came sauntering in, looking extremely pleased with himself. 'I have returned with our means of transport as promised.'

He came over and bent to remove the gag. Amelia coughed and spat on the floor, relieved to be rid of that at least. As she opened her mouth to retort, he put up a hand. 'No screaming now, unless you wish me to hurt you?' This was said almost hopefully, and Amelia shuddered again, closing her mouth.

'Nothing to say? How unusual,' Bernard drawled. 'Well, perhaps this will get you talking – I will ruin you. That way your husband won't want you back, even if he does catch up with us.'

'My lord, I've seen him!'

Bootle had come rushing up the front steps of the house, just as James had been about to leave on yet another search of grounds.

'Sir Bernard? Where?'

'In the village.' Bootle was struggling to catch his breath, his face red with exertion. 'He was talking to a rum fellow, and eventually he went off with him. I followed discreetly, and it turns out he was hiring a horse and carriage.'

'And where is he now?'

James was almost jumping up and down with impatience.

They had not a moment to lose if the stupid fellow had a carriage.

'He set off in the opposite direction, out of the village, and I came here as fast as I could.'

'Thank you, you'd better have a rest now. We'll go after him and see if we can pick up a trail. There was no sign of Amelia?'

'No, my lord.'

'Then he must have hidden her somewhere. Let's go!' he bellowed to the men already waiting with horses saddled, and the group set off at high speed. When they reached the village they went in search of the man Grigson, who was the only one who could have rented out a horse and carriage as far as James knew, and the man soon told them all he knew.

'Said he'd been staying in an old barn last night, as he'd had an accident with his own carriage. I'm guessing he meant the one over by Farmer Jacobs'.'

'Of course. Many thanks.'

James knew the place well and cursed himself for not thinking of it earlier. The ride there took no more than a few minutes, but they were the longest minutes in his life.

As Bernard came closer, Amelia tried desperately to think of some way of deterring him.

'Why would you want me now?' she asked scornfully. 'I've been married for months and my husband isn't exactly a monk.'

Bernard frowned, his euphoria evaporating temporarily, but then he smiled. 'To be sure, I would rather have been your first lover, my dear, but maidens are rather tedious. I'm sure you will make a much more exciting mistress.' He put one arm around her and began to paw her with the other. When he bent to kiss her, she twisted her head away.

'If you want me to put up a spirited defence, shouldn't you untie my hands?' she said, trying not to let the desperation show in her voice.

Bernard stopped what he was doing and smiled again, a wolfish grin that was beginning to make Amelia feel nauseous. 'Do you know, I believe you're right? Don't think you'll be able to get away though, my strength is vastly superior to yours and I'm wise to your little tricks now.'

He pulled out a small pocket knife and reached around her to cut through the rope. All too soon, however, he began the assault again.

Amelia tried everything she could think of to defend herself, but he had been right in saying that he was too strong. She managed to escape his clutches once and bolted for the door, but he was too fast and caught her in an instant. He backhanded her viciously so that her head swam. Amelia thought her battle was lost for certain, but just then the door flew open and James burst in, followed by several other men.

'You beast!' James lifted Bernard bodily off Amelia and slammed him into the wall. He stood before the man; fury blazing out of his ice-blue eyes and Amelia noticed with satisfaction that Bernard no longer looked quite so cocky. 'Well, coward, are you going to stand up and fight me or do you only fight women?' James taunted.

Bernard flushed a dull red and charged at his opponent, but the fight that followed was very one-sided. Amelia knew that James had trained at the famous Gentleman Jackson's boxing salon, whereas years of soft living had done nothing for Bernard's fitness. In the end, he made a run for the door and James let him go.

'If you so much as come near my wife again, I'll have you before a magistrate so fast you won't know what hit you!' he shouted after him. 'Don't think I don't mean it.'

Bernard scrambled on to his horse and galloped off as if all the hounds of hell were after him.

'Amelia, my love, are you all right? Did he hurt you? I should have killed him, shouldn't I?'

'I'm fine, James,' Amelia said shakily. 'Truly, you came in time.'

He sat down on the floor next to her and took her in his arms and Amelia leaned her head on his shoulders. It felt so good, sitting there like that, safe and happy, and she never wanted to move.

'How did you find me?' she asked.

'I had men out searching for you and Bootle saw your cousin trying to hire a conveyance. After that, it was fairly easy.' He pulled her closer. 'I thought I would go mad with worry. I love you Amelia. Can you forgive me for my idiotic behaviour yesterday? I was only trying to protect you by not telling you about Sir Bernard's threats, but I realise now that I shouldn't have kept you in the dark.'

'Of course I forgive you. I love you too, have done almost from the first moment, I think.' She looked up at him and smiled.

'I don't deserve you, you know,' he said, cupping her cheek with one hand. 'You are altogether too good to be true. I'm sorry I ever doubted you, but my first wife made me mistrustful and I believed all women to be the same. I'm glad you've proved me wrong.'

He stood up and bent to lift her into his arms. 'And now we'd better return home.'

'Home, how truly wonderful that sounds.'

'Yes, and it's all thanks to you – you've made Marr Place into a real home for a happy family, and that's how we shall remain.'

The following summer saw Holt House opened up to guests for the first time in years, as the old Earl had invited as many people as the place could hold for the christening of his new grandson, who to his great joy had been named after him. He sat in a chair in the middle of the room, beaming at all and sundry.

'You look to be in great health, Grandfather,' James commented during a lull in the proceedings.

'Never better, my boy, thanks to you.'

'And what happened to being at death's door?'

'Oh, that.' The old man shrugged his shoulders. 'Sometimes little white lies are necessary in order to get what you want and my memory isn't what it used to be. I get confused.'

James shook his head at him and smiled. 'Pah! You're incorrigible, but since you helped me to find happiness, I'll forgive you this time.'

The publishers hope that this book has given you enjoyable reading. Large Print Books are especially designed to be as easy to see and hold as possible. If you wish a complete list of our books please ask at your local library or write directly to:

Dales Large Print Books
Magna House, Long Preston,
Skipton, North Yorkshire.
BD23 4ND